THE DARK PLANET

THE OBSIDIAN SPINDLE SAGA
BOOK TWELVE

RUSSELL NOHELTY

SPECIAL THANKS

Talinda Willard, HyliaKumatora, Chris Roeszler, Amy Teegan, Chip Orlikowski, RHR, Victoria Nohelty, Alexander Joyner, Pierino Gattei, Caspar Williams, Gerald P. McDaniel, Walter Weiss, Sunny Side Up, Kenny Endlich, Amber Reeves, Joshua Bowers, Elias Rosner, Noah Carruba, John "AcesofDeath7" Mullens, Jamie Minnich, Rowan Stone, Taiga Char, BAOCHAU TRAN, Jeff Lewis, Dave Baxter, Chad Bowden, David Irgang, James Kralik, Emerson Kasak, Matthew Johnson, Paul Rose Jr., Shannon, Dr. Charles Elbert Norton III, Edward Nycz Jr., Jessica Meuth, Caledonia, GMarkC, Chris Cheek, Bianca Tatjana Višić Ritorto, John Otway Jr, Brett Bennett, Jason 'XenoPhage' Frisvold, Scott Chisholm, Amanda Sarah, Alexandra Corrsin, Giles Fox, Rick Parker, H, Rob Steinberger, Alec Loases, David Stephenson, Anthony James Frandsen, JohnDoe, Joshua Easter, MadCatter (Cat Fleming), Kevin Potter, Bill Lisse, Michael Szewczyk, Robert Woods Tienken, Ronald L Weston, Karen Haughn, Shem Bingman, Susan Wilson, Brigitte Ziegler, Matt Soucy, Alyssa, Michelle Pelo, Richard A Shirley, PerryC, Elizabeth Kiefer, Tim, Nicolas Mandujano

III, Karen Roads, Rhel ná DecVandé, Zeb Berryman, Al Gonzalez, S. D., Jörn Flath, Rick Radzville, Aaron Loren, Justise Briones(That/Them), Genevieve Slunka, Michael DeCarlo, Kitty Crab, Jeanne L. Warner, Vi Ta, Bridget D Laurent, Jaime Bialer, Wendy Martinez, Nicholas Harezga, Mira Hunter, Cara Reasner, Lori Case, Melevorn, Rebecca Hill, Jane R., Talia Denham, Jordan Harju, Jesse Coe, Greg Levick, and Andrew Messiah.

The Dark Planet
Book 12 of the Obsidian Spindle Saga

By:
Russell Nohelty

Edited by:
Leah Lederman

Proofread by:
Katrina Roets

Cover by:
JV Arts

Formatting by:
Turbo Kitten Industries

CHAPTER I
CHELLE

Rama sat in the middle of the shack we'd reached through a series of poorly made tunnels beneath the main city of Kadlu's acid rain drenched world. The sky had been torched in a battle between the gods, and the whole population was driven underground, so there probably weren't minor and major cities anymore, just ones that survived...and ones that didn't. If the living conditions of these people were any indication, it wasn't much of a victory to survive. They did it out of sheer stubbornness. I understood that. I lived, died, and came back again based on sheer stubbornness mixed with a hefty dash of spite.

What mattered was that this was the city closest to the Obsidian Spindle, and a Spindle could travel a million miles in a matter of seconds.

Upon entering the Dream Realm what felt like a hundred years ago, and becoming a Fate after the death of Atropos, I thought the Obsidian Spindle situated behind the Emerald City was the most important object in the whole universe, used to commune with the Fates and return to Earth from the world of Urgu. I treated it with disproportionate reverence and awe, but I learned quickly that there were thousands of Obsidian Spindles spread throughout the universe.

More than that—they were little more than a travel network set up by the gods. The Obsidian Spindle was utilitarian, no more magical than taking a plane. You wouldn't hold reverence for one of those unless you were an idiot.

To be fair, if you went back even a century, the thought of the average human being able to cut through the sky and reach from New York to London in a matter of hours instead of days or weeks would have been a fantasy akin to traveling between worlds. But now plane travel had become a mundane reality of our existence, just like the Obsidian Spindles had become to me. The only thing that retained its awe to me in the whole universe was Rose.

"Hey," Rose said as she caught my stare and walked toward me, swinging her hips. "Why are you looking at me like that?"

Rose had only been gifted with the god's magic for a short time, but she absolutely flourished with their blessing. It made me wonder if she needed me at all. We met when the both of us were poor and piteous, and I remained that way while she became a formidable force in the universe. She was a true steward of the universe, helping to bend it toward justice; all I was good for was getting captured and putting her in danger.

"Nothing," I said, shaking my head. "I just think that what you've done is amazing. You saved Rama, and—"

"Hey," she said forcefully but kindly. "We saved him together. Odin would have cut us down if you didn't come for me."

"Maybe. Honestly, I think you would have figured out a way out." I sighed. "That's just the way you are." I looked back at Kadlu and Rama, sitting next to each other. I felt their love for each other all the way across the room.

As far as I was concerned, the universe was shaped by those with a strong will and dogged determination to grab the timeline of history and twist it to their whims. The arc of history listed towards cruelty if anything, because the gods were cruel.

I wasn't wrong. Kadlu taught me that a group of uninspired gods—the Board—had created everything in existence and were entrusted with the day-to-day minutiae of running the universe. They'd tilted the scales to favor the despots they held in their own image. There could be no justice until the Board had been unseated from power...and that was not even our biggest problem.

The Spore was our biggest problem.

Rose smiled at me. "Oh, so you're throwing yourself a pity party over here. I was wondering why you've been so distant."

"I'm not holding a—" I bit my tongue when I realized she was right. "Okay, maybe just a little pity party."

She placed her hand gently on my arm. "We've saved each other enough times that I thought we got over keeping score."

I dropped my head, unable to meet her eyes. "It's just—I hate feeling like a damsel in distress."

She laughed. "Well, yeah, being that kind of person sucks, but you're not that. After all, this whole craziness started with you saving me."

I sucked in a breath of air. "Yeah, but since then you've gotten blessed by two gods and all I've been able to do is die and get captured."

"Wasn't it you who told me not to feel bad for not being the most powerful girl in the world—and that the only thing that mattered was what you thought of me?" She grabbed my hands and squeezed them.

"Yeah," I said softly. "I guess so."

Rose laid her head on my shoulder. "And do you remember what you told me?"

"No."

I felt her smile even though I couldn't see it. "You told me that I was the most important person in the world to you, and as long as that was true, and that you were the most important person in the world to me, then nothing else mattered. You told me that as long as that was true, we were the most powerful people in the whole universe."

I furrowed my brow. "Are you sure I said that? It sounds a little more cheeseball than I have the ability to be."

"Maybe I'm editorializing a bit, but that was the gist." She sat up and looked me in the eyes. "So, I ask you, Chelle, love of my life and light of my heart, am I still the most important person in the world to you?"

I squeezed her hand hard. "Of course. Always and forever."

"Good," she said with a small smile. "Because you are the most important person to me, which means that we're together, and that's all that matters in all of this."

I looked over at Kadlu. "I think your new friend would very much say saving the universe is the most important thing."

"Without you, I would never have the courage to save the universe. All the strength I have, that I have ever had, is because of you." Rose nodded at Rama. "I think he's ready to tell us what he knows. Are you going to come listen, or do you want to mope over here like a little baby?"

"That was such a sweet moment and you ruined it."

"Tough love, baby. You gotta take the sugar with the salt."

I leaned forward and kissed her. "I take it all, forever. Now, come on. I think I'm done with my pity party. Let's go save the world."

CHAPTER 2
RED

I spent so much time trying to find Nimue, and by extension the Dark Planet, that I never thought of what it would be like on the other side of the great locked door. The first thing I felt when I came through was a gust of cold, bitter air. It reeked like the sweat that dripped off of the tortured souls in the Underworld, where all hope was lost and all that remained was doom. I shuddered, recalling the piteous cries of the condemned.

I set my feet down in a thick forest among gnarled trees that braided their bark together to form a leafless canopy. When the forest finally broke into a field, I realized that even if there had been easy sight of the sky, there would not have been a star in the sky close enough to produce the light needed to create daylight. In fact, even as I strained my eyes to their limit, I could not make out one single light in the sky. Now I knew why they called it the Dark Planet, and why the only things that could exist on it were the twisted, horrible creatures that thrived in the darkness.

"It is not all so bad as that," Nox said, grinning at the look on my face. She had curled up in a tight cross-legged pose with her hands held tight against her knees. "Beauty grows in the darkness, too. That is what the gods you worship never understood."

"How is it possible for them to deny the darkness?" I asked, sitting down next to her. "I have been to the Celestial Realm, and there is barely a light in the sky. You would think they would honor the darkness as well as the light."

She shook her head. "There is so little you understand."

"Then quit treating me like a child and explain it. I may not understand, but I can learn."

"Very well." She took a deep breath, luxuriating in the same harsh air that turned my stomach. "The first thing you must know is that the gods would never accept any light that burned brighter than themselves, and letting a star burn too close would dim their presence, or so their feeble brains believe."

"That much I understand, but that is not the whole story."

"No, it is not. The gods, or at least those you call gods, were not the first to rule the universe. Your Nox was not the first god of darkness. In fact, the one who came before was ridiculed when she chose to rule the shadows of the universe, but she knew the truth...that true power, true beauty, rested in the abyss." Nox gestured around her. "Without the darkness, the universe would be a millionth its size, small enough to be crushed in my hand. Dark matter is everything, and yet the gods fear it, and by extension, humanity fears it."

"Then you must love the Celestial Realm."

"We did not call it that, when it was ours." She looked out into the middle distance. "My people...they lived at the center of the universe once, where your Celestial Realm now resides. Even the gods could not deny its power after they kicked out the rightful rulers, banishing us to the furthest reaches of the universe, a place outside of time and space, where they expected my brethren to die."

"But they—you—did not die?" I asked.

"I hope not, but I truly do not know."

I took a deep breath. "And you have taken over Nox's body, but you are not her, right?"

"Correct. I am not the Nox you knew, though I retain her memories." The creature placed a smile on the god's face. "I am glad we can drop the charade. Those that know better call us the Spore."

"Is she dead? Nox?"

The creature I knew as Nox shook her head. "Not quite. She can hear everything we are saying, but she is not, as they say on your planet, 'in the driver's seat.' We have lived in many gods, and Nox is easily the most difficult to control. Perhaps it is because she loves the dark as much as we do. I almost think we could have been friends if our aims were aligned more closely."

"Friends don't take over each other's bodies."

"Your friends, maybe," she said. "But yours is only one way of being, and it is not a very pleasant existence, truth be told. Where I am from, we live together as one; individually and together, as one. That is what we created this universe to be, but your gods had other plans."

"And you hope to bring your friends back from beyond the universe and punish the gods for their insolence?"

"It is more than that." Nox looked at me, but her eyes stared right through me. "Do you ever feel that this universe was not meant for you? Perhaps that you are fighting against a greater truth, or that existence should not be so difficult as you make it out to be?"

"I do, but then, I am not from around here."

"No, you are not. You are special—a beautiful abomination, like me."

I sneered. "We are nothing alike. You aim to destroy the universe, and I work to save it."

"You are wrong." Her eyes went cold. "This universe is not yours to control. It was meant for my people, and it was taken from us. You are simply parasites that have grown comfortable here. The universe is dying because you are not taking care of it, because you have no idea how to be good stewards of the life that we intended to thrive. Instead, you call it hideous, when it is truly the most beautiful thing in existence, made in the image of the gods that wanted them to rule the universe, not you. The only reason you continue to flourish in this place is because the gods fight against entropy to keep it so. You, and the gods that made you, are parasites, and I aim to exterminate you for the good of the universe."

I shook my head, baffled. "I'm not going to allow you to destroy the universe, even if you think you're trying to save it."

Nox smiled. "That is what I like most about you, human. You refuse to go quiet into oblivion. If you were not so important, I would show you the truth right now, but..."

She trailed off, and my face turned sour. "What does that mean?"

Nox inhaled deeply as she stood. "This is how the universe should smell. I am happy that at least one place was able to find the equilibrium we intended."

"You didn't answer my question."

"Enough, parasite," she snapped. "I've only given you this information because it would be cruel to send you to fulfill your purpose without knowing a small morsel of the truth."

"You say that like I will help you."

Her smile was unnatural. "You will whether you want to or not, but now you must make a choice. Come with me willingly to gather what I need from this place and face your nemesis head on...or fight me here and now. You'll learn how futile it is to fight your betters and lose what little agency I have given you."

I snarled, but then I bit my lip. Nox was powerful, and this being controlling her must be even more so. I needed to bide my time, feign complicity, and wait for my moment to strike.

"You speak of Nimue," I said. "She is the nemesis I seek."

"Indeed."

"If you aim to bring me to her, then I will come with you, as long as you allow me to kill her without interference."

"It amuses me that you think to bargain with me, but fear not, I will not interfere with your heart's desire. You have my word on that, for what that is worth to you."

"Then I will come with you, for now."

"You have made a wise choice." She put a hand on my shoulder. "The other way would have been less than pleasant."

CHAPTER 3
ARIEL

I knew something bad had happened before I even opened my eyes, because when I tried to stretch and wipe the sleep from my face, I found myself bound tightly. I was in a sterile, circular room with three metal beds in its center.

A large, silver box stood blinking on the far end of the room, connected by different colored ropes to each of the beds. A large dome overhead had a hole in the center to let a large rod poke through into the dark, starry sky.

"You're up," a hoarse voice whispered.

Hypnos was bound next to me, his arms and legs splayed and wrapped with thick leather against a slab similar of polished metal. I didn't know something so simple could hold a god, but he had been captured by Nox, and—

The last days came flooding back to me. Traveling to the Nightmare Realm to find Rapunzel's eye, then to a dark castle on a high mountain, being saved by a dark king who turned out to be a scared child—and then returning to the Dream Realm to find those I promised protection in Hypnos's bosom slaughtered. They'd been dusted by Nox, who had a wild look in her eye and an unconscious Hypnos crumpled at her side.

"You're alive!" I shouted. "Praise the gods."

Hypnos had a bitter look on his face, the usual pink hue of his eyes replaced by a dull brown. "Don't praise my brethren. They are not to thank for my salvation."

"Very true," a voice chimed in as a door slid open. A god wearing a shimmering blue medallion, every hair on his head white and kissed by the finest silk, walked into the room. His eyes were black as ink and so was his tongue. "My mistress sends her regards. She hoped to meet you when you returned, but she has been called away on pressing business, so you were left in my care."

"And who are you?" I asked.

"My kind do not like names, but you call us the Spore. Even saying that name tastes bitter on this one's tongue. You may call me Ukko, or Spore, or nothing. I prefer the latter."

"Ukko was one on the Board," Hypnos said. "I recognize that name, and his face."

Ukko held out his arms and studied them. "Yes, this body was a member of the Board. It satisfied our needs for a time, but recent development has forced us to change tactics."

"Wait," I replied, a raging pain in my forehead. "The Board? I have never heard of such a thing during all my time in the Dream Realm."

"Because you are not in the Dream Realm," Hypnos growled. "You have been made corporeal by my mother's dark magic, no doubt as some part of her diabolical plan."

Not in the Dream Realm? Corporeal? That meant my body had been rendered back unto the universe for the first time in three hundred years. I sniffed the air, and it was sweet, unlike the nothing I'd grown used to since my soul had been resurrected in the Dream Realm. *Could such a miracle be true?*

"I don't understand. How?"

Ukko smiled. "It is old magic, for sure. When my kind ruled the world, it was very common. Everything, in its way, is energy made corporeal. It just hasn't been seen in many generations because the gods have bastardized our powers."

I frowned. "What are you talking about?"

"Of course, you are only human, which means you have feeble minds." Ukko looked at Hypnos. "Do you want to tell her, since you created them?"

"If it shuts you up." Hypnos sighed. "Several billion years ago, the universe was created in a flurry of energy by the Primordials. They are older than time itself, and when they grew tired of an endless eternity filled with nothingness, they turned to a new project, creating a universe they could mold to their wills. Eventually, in their dabbling, they created the first gods, who birthed more and more."

"One of our worst ideas." Ukko visibly shuddered. "For soon enough, their vanity got the better of them, and the gods decided they should be in charge. We were more powerful, but they were numerous, like viruses, and they pushed us back to the edge of the universe and bound us there."

I looked over at Hypnos. "Is that true?"

"It's true. They wanted to turn existence into—" His face twisted in a way that I had never seen, filled with anger and contempt. He cleared his throat. "We did not agree with their twisted view of the universe."

"It was our universe to twist to our wills!" Ukko shouted. He paused and collected himself. "This is the vanity I'm referring to, and it still courses through your veins, but no bother. Time is nothing to us, and in short order we will make right the things that were once put wrong."

A kernel of understanding blinked across my mind, and then vanished. When I couldn't quite piece it together, Hypnos growled at Ukko. "They aim to open the barrier that exists between us and them, and take back what we took from them, bringing forth an era of horror on this universe that you cannot even imagine."

I did not like the sound of that. "No. You can't."

"Yes, we can do anything, that is the point." Ukko smiled an odd smile. "You cannot stop us. Far from it."

"I can try." I wriggled unsuccessfully against my restraints.

"You will fail, but you are welcome to try. Perhaps you might even stall us for a moment, but then you will take your place in our grand plan."

"I want no part in your sick games," I spat back.

"That is not your choice. You will help usher in a new age whether you like to or not, and then, the universe will be ours."

CHAPTER 4

ROSE

Chelle was a husk of her former self after being captured and tortured by Odin. I was so grateful to Red for rescuing my sweet love, but I wished she had gotten there sooner. Now, Chelle spent most of her time staring off into space and bristling at my touch.

I tried to tell her that she was my savior as much as I was hers, but she couldn't get it through her thick skull that we were a team. We wouldn't stand a chance of saving the universe without her, and she saved me every day by simply existing.

The thought of it gave me the slightest smile, and Chelle cocked her head as she looked at me. "What are you thinking about?"

My smile grew. "Us, together, with all this drama behind us, being able to live out our lives in blissful peace."

She laughed. "Do you really think you can go back to a simple life after everything you've seen?"

"I don't know, but all of this nonsense makes me want a quiet existence even more. Maybe I won't be able to stand it, but I look forward to finding out when we win."

"If we win," Kadlu said, rubbing Rama's back. "Which is a big if."

"I know," I replied. "Forgive me for being optimistic for a moment. You do remember I saved several realms before, right? It's not my first rodeo, and every time it's always darkest in the moments before we summon our courage and win the day."

"You've never seen anything like the Spore before," Rama said.

"Yeah, we've heard that before, too," Chelle said, crouching on the floor next to the two of them. "We've never beaten the new big bad, until we do."

I joined them in their circle, and together the four of us looked at each other. Finally, Kadlu turned to Rama and spoke. "Are you ready?"

Rama shivered. "I think so. I'm sorry for being so quiet for the last couple of days. The Spore...their memories live inside my brain, but they come as flashes, jumbled. The further I get from them, the less I remember. But I think I know their plan."

"Tell us already! I want to get out of this gods-forsaken shack." Chelle glanced at Kadlu. "No offense."

Kadlu smiled. "No need to apologize. The gods have indeed forsaken it, and this planet, which is why I like it so much."

"Maybe we should let Rama speak," I said, squeezing Chelle's leg. "This must be hard for him."

She looked down. "I'm sorry for the interruption. It's been a crazy couple of days—for all of us, I guess."

"It's okay," Rama replied, taking a deep breath. "Okay, here we go. The Spore are one of ten immortal beings that created the universe, including the gods and nearly everything else in existence. At first the gods were a small piece of the universe, made as a curiosity more than anything, but over time they grew in power, finding ways to siphon the magic from the Primordials themselves."

"The Primordials?" I frowned.

Rama looked at our confused faces. "That is what they called themselves, and honestly, even the Spore did not know much more than that, and I was one of them. They simply went from *not* being...to being. If there is a better explanation, they did not know it."

"What do they want?" I asked.

"What anyone wants who has been separated by those they love—to be reunited with their family."

Chelle shrugged. "That doesn't sound so bad."

"Believe me when I tell you it is." A look of horror rose on his face. "You have no idea the sick, twisted things the Primordials want to do with the universe. The Dark Planet is only a taste of their warped minds. If they are allowed to return to reclaim their throne, then the Nightmare Realm will become the norm, and they will wipe humanity out of existence. The gods, too."

Kadlu swallowed. "That doesn't sound good."

"It's worse than anything you can imagine," Rama said. "And the Spore have waited an eternity to enact their plans, slowly weaseling their way into power, and getting in the right position so that when the opportunity arose, they would be ready to strike."

"And why do they think now is the time?" Chelle asked.

"Because of you, actually," Rama said. "And your friend, Gabrielle. Nox created you from the energy of the universe. Gods have many tricks up their sleeve, but that kind of magic has always been reserved for the Primordials themselves. Even the Spore could not do it, as their power rested in infecting others, and they were limited to the abilities their hosts could provide."

I dug my nails into Chelle's thigh until she winced in pain. I hadn't meant to hurt her, but I was shaking so badly with fear that I needed an anchor. "What do they want to do with Chelle?"

"To use her, like a battery, to fuel a machine that can slice open the barrier holding the Primordials back. Now, all they need are three bodies created from the magic of the Dream Realm and incarnated into flesh to power the machine. They know of Chelle and Gabrielle. When I was cut off from the Source, they were headed to find a third suitable candidate in the Dream Realm, someone named Ariel. Once they have those three, and Rapunzel's body, there will be no stopping them."

I leaned forward. "Then we will make sure they never get her no matter how long we have to fight."

"It is much worse than that. The Spore are not one, or ten, or a hundred." Rama swallowed loudly. "In my short time on the Board, I was able to infect the other members, and poison the water supply so that any god who drank the water would fall under their thrall. It is only a matter of time before they find us here and attack. Every single one of them."

As if on cue, the shack rumbled. I rushed for the door, but I didn't need to see outside to know what had happened. The Spore were coming for us.

CHAPTER 5
NIMUE

I should be happy. The King in Yellow was dead. His reign of terror, the scourge of the Dark Planet, ended by the combined power of Rapunzel, Elvira, Cassandra, Lydia, Bethel, Delilah, Baba, and me. And yet, my heart was heavy. Too many died in the process of killing Hastur. Elvira never even made it back from the mad witch's prison, and now Baba used my sister's skin as her own. Rapunzel lay in two pieces on either side of the crumbled castle, and when all hope seemed lost, Bethel gave her life to deliver the fatal blow.

I had knelt over her body for a long time, crying until I had no more tears to give, as the other princesses and Baba looked on in disgust. Even in the saddest moments, they believed that showing emotion was a weakness. Maybe I was weak. Only Cassandra, the woman who betrayed me on my first meeting with the dark king, knelt next to me and allowed herself to feel the sadness of our combined loss.

"It's okay," she whispered, rubbing my back as I heaved uncontrollably.

I had not known Bethel for long, and our meetings were terse and fraught with antipathy, but she died to save us all, and in my long life few had ever risked themselves so that I might live.

"She died well," Cassandra said. "Which is a far bit better than living poorly."

"And she has allowed us to usher in a new age for the Dark Planet," Delilah added. "Though, admittedly, my faith in your leadership wanes with each moment of this...display."

I didn't care if I looked weak, or pathetic. I had no interest in leading the Dark Planet. I had every intention of saying my goodbyes to the princesses and taking my leave. However, as I bent down to say one last goodbye to the woman that gave everything so that we could live free, wave after wave of emotion crashed upon me, and I suddenly felt everything that I had once been too numb, or too scared, to feel for myself.

Eventually the tears dried up and I wiped my eyes with the alabaster hands given to me by my betrothed, cracked with black with shimmering stars illuminating the darkness. I had thought that Hastur's magic might dispel the power he'd cast upon us all, but it remained.

A puddle of black bile had gathered at my feet. What had leaked from my eyes were not tears but a black oil that slowly funneled down to a drain in the middle of the floor.

"Are you done?" Lydia asked, a galaxy spinning where her head should have been. Her words were not spoken but bored into my head, and the heads of all those around her.

"I believe so," I replied. "Thank you for waiting."

"We didn't do it for you," Baba said. "You have abdicated your claim to the throne, but instead of giving it to me, you offered it to these abominations that have no more right to rule than I have to eat the moon."

"We were the princesses anointed by the previous king," Delilah growled. "The right to rule passes to us."

"Please," Baba growled. "You were his playthings. He only called you princesses because 'concubine' would have sullied his impenetrable ego."

"No," Delilah snarled. "He gave us responsibility to act in his stead multiple times and in countless situations. We were his eyes, and his fists, when he couldn't be there himself. If any deserve to rule, it is us."

Baba squared her shoulders defiantly. The sight of her wearing the skin of Elvira, her white skin and six horns under the control of the sorceress boiled my blood and sobered my mind.

"I made a deal with you, Baba, to give Hastur's crown to you. And I have delivered my promise. I never promised to deliver you the throne"—I pointed to the broken and splintered chair—"but there it rests. You can take it for yourself, but the right to rule was never mine to give. It belongs to these women who fought alongside you, and if you cannot figure this out peacefully, I am very sure they are prepared to defend their position."

"This is a betrayal of the highest order," Baba cried. "I will send you to my dungeons, where the beasts I keep will have their way with you."

Delilah stepped in front of me. "And you will do so by going through me."

Cassandra took a menacing step forward. "And me."

Finally, Lydia joined the other princesses. "You will have to face us all, Baba, and we will take no pity on you just because you wear our sister's skin."

"You would defend this wretch?" Baba spat, gesturing

in my direction. "Look at her. She weeps like a baby at the sight of death."

"It is a wretched sight." Delilah glared at me. "But she is our wretch, and we only had the strength to stand against Hastur because she taught us how to work together."

"A tough lesson to learn," Lydia added, her voice echoing through my skull. "But one we took to quite well, and now that we have learned its power, we will use it to stand against you, and any others that wish us harm."

"You are more than welcome to fight us for the throne," Cassandra said. "But you will not find us shrinking violets, or easy targets, a lesson your progeny learned the hard way."

"My son sat on the throne," Baba growled. "As such, the line of succession falls to me."

"That might be," I replied. "But the only way you will take it back is by force, and I know you now, Baba. You claim to be a powerful witch, but you are a coward. You chose to live in the shadows rather than challenge Hastur. You cower from any confrontation with any who have the power to challenge you, and only lord it over those who cannot defend themselves. I have known others like you, and the only thing I am sure of is that you do not have the will to challenge us."

The old witch stomped forward until she was nose to nose with me. "I saved you! Without me you would have lost!"

Cassandra nodded. "You're right, which is why I would like to offer you my piece of the throne."

"No," Delilah said. "You can't—"

"It is mine to do with what I choose. Nimue abdicated her responsibility to us, and I abdicate mine to Baba, but only if she can play nicely with the others, and accept her place in the fold, instead of demanding to rule it."

Baba snarled. "The crown is mine!"

"And it means nothing without the power to rule," Delilah said. "The power that only rests through us, and Nimue is right. I see it in your eyes now. My sister never showed fear, but I see it bubbling up in you."

Lydia stood straight. "You do not deserve to wear her skin or wield her power, but I cannot deny Cassandra the right to give her power to whomever she chooses. Too long were we told what we must do, and I will not do the same, no matter how much I disagree with her decision."

The earth moved, and a burst of dark energy exploded in the center of the room. When it dissipated, Nox stood between us, smiling. She looked all around, and then her eyes found Rapunzel's mangled body.

"Ah, there she is." Her eyes found mine. "I'll be taking that now, if you please."

CHAPTER 6

ARIEL

"So, you aim to kill me then," I asked, less frightened by my fate than resigned to it.

"Sacrifice you for the greatest good is how I would put it," Ukko replied. "There can be no greater purpose than this, but I've said too much already. I will let the master host speak to that."

"What are you talking about? What master host?"

He fell silent and busied himself with the many cords and buttons flashing around the room. He took great care in polishing every surface until they glimmered, and I could see myself reflected in them, but he did not speak again no matter how much I pressed him to answer my questions.

I had never thought myself pretty, but I believed I had an understated elegance that came with being the daughter of a queen. I had never turned away from my reflection until I saw it reflected by the instruments of my doom. The lush red curls that I loved so much had frayed and split. My white skin had grown pasty, and dark circles dug deep into the area under my eyes. I was merely a shadow of a woman I once recognized.

When Ukko finally left the room, I turned to Hypnos. "We have to get out of here."

"It's impossible. These restraints were meant to keep even the most powerful god at bay. We have no chance at breaking them."

"How can you say that? I've seen you do incredible things. You are as powerful as any god."

He sucked at his teeth. "In the Dream Realm, maybe, but here, in the real world, what I can do is barely more than a magician performing party tricks at children's birthdays."

An idea came to me. "If the Dream Realm is where you are most powerful, then we must go there."

Hypnos shook his head. "If I could get to the Dream Realm, I would already be there, but these restraints bind me to this place, constricting my powers through immense pain at even the most minor use."

It took me another moment to come up with a second idea. "Then send me."

"It won't work, either. I can't—well...wait. Maybe... maybe I could send your consciousness into the Dream Realm, but it will be incredibly painful to fight through the restraints for both of us. Are you sure you are up for it?"

I nodded. "If the only other choice is to become a sacrificial lamb in a foolish quest to destroy the universe, then I will take pain to mitigate that fate every time."

"I doubt you will save your fate, but you might be able to save the Dream Realm."

"Why would Urgu be in danger?"

"Nox found us in the Dream Realm and stole us from there. If she could do that, then she could have brought any amount of agony onto my domain." He lowered his voice. "Listen to me. You must make it to Nox's keep under the sea. Inside her vault there is a sword with the name 'Hope Bringer' formed in elvish on the hilt. You must bring it to the castle and place it in a hidden slot under the throne. Do this, and I stand a chance of breaking these chains. Do this, and the Dream Realm has a chance of surviving."

"I will do anything to save the Dream Realm."

"May the gods bless you."

His eyes glowed their usual bright pink for one moment. He bit his lip hard to contain his pained screams and a surge of power rippled from the tip of my nose through the front of my skull, down to my fingers and toes. When it reached the back of my skull, my body spasmed, throwing my head back until it cracked against the back of the metal holding me down, and I fell unconscious.

Pink wisps, tendrils from the deep wrapped around my arms and legs, yanking me downward into a pool of tar, which seeped up my body and worked against the light to pull me away. Everywhere it touched me, pins and needles pierced through my skin and into the core of my being. I thought of letting go of the pain and letting it consume me, but then a wave of resolution took hold.

No. I will not succumb.

I reached my hands upward, fighting the ichor. An electrical shock fired through me, and I nearly lost my hold on the pink wisps. With the last of my strength, I pulled myself up out of the tar and when I did, the pink light shot me forward until I smashed into a wall of whiteness. I heard a crash, and then I fell, down, down, down, until I crashed into the hard ground.

When my eyes focused again, I was in the Emerald City, the castle rising high above me, and the sound of screams echoing through the streets.

CHAPTER 7
NIMUE

"The hell you are!" I shouted as Nox approached Rapunzel's body. I had thought the Faceless Woman so strong, but she only withstood a few seconds against Hastur. Now her head and torso were on one side of me and her legs on the other. I was glad I didn't fall deeper into her thrall, but she did not deserve to die in such a horrible manner.

Nox grinned as she kept coming forward, revealing a woman in a red cape behind her. *Red.* I never thought I would see her again.

"You have upgraded the company you keep, Red," I said with a smile.

Red looked around at the princesses and Baba. "And you have downgraded yours. I always knew you were a monster, but now you look the part, Nimue."

"Hey!" Cassandra shouted. "Don't you—"

"I can handle one indignant whelp." I held up my hand to stay her words. "Don't judge them too harshly, Red. Just because they don't look like perfect dolls doesn't make them monsters. As for me, I am what the gods made me:

beautiful, powerful, iconic, and perfect. Finally, after eons of cowing to power, I finally discovered my own."

Nox stepped between us when Red pulled two daggers out of her belt. "This is cute, but really, I'm in a rush. I don't really care how you opened the door, but I thank you for doing it."

"Great queen," Baba said, kneeling in front of her. "We hid the key in my son's body, and with his death, you have come to us as foretold."

Nox's lip curled. "I don't like you."

The god placed her hand on Baba's head, and it exploded out in a hundred different directions as if it were filled with dynamite. Blood and viscera shot on all of us, but we had seen too much by that point to even bat an eye.

"Thank you," Delilah said. "She was insufferable."

Nox waved her hand, and the brains splattered on her flowing black dress vanished. "Now that you see what I do to those who prostrate themselves before me, let me assure you that I do much worse to those that defy me."

"We have taken down one god this day," Delilah said. "We have no problem taking down a second."

"A god? That's cute. I am so much more than that." She leaned forward. "We do not have to be enemies. You are the perfect creations we intended when we made this universe. Once I open the door to my brethren, you will be welcomed into our new vision, instead of cast out like the bastard stepchild you are now."

"You can't be serious," Red said. "If this is the kind of thing you intend to let exist in the same universe as me, then I will have no part in helping you."

Nox snapped her fingers and Red rose into the air, bound by inky black restraints that appeared out of nothing. When she opened her mouth to scream, Nox bound her mouth.

"She does go on, doesn't she?"

"You don't know the half of it." I rolled my eyes, and then fixed them on Nox again. This was not the goddess I knew. That Nox was directionless and content to waste away under the sea in the precious realm she'd built. The one standing before me now was somehow more confident, but also more focused. She wanted something grander, and in that, I felt we understood each other.

"Now, about my offer..." She trailed off, letting the words linger on the air.

I cocked my head to the side. "I'm listening."

She stepped between us all, and the princesses parted for her. "Too long the gods have gone against the divine will of the universe, twisting our intention, turning what was once beautiful, ugly; what was once ugly, beautiful. This is the time to rise up and take your place among the rightful rulers of this universe and sit at our right hand as we forge a path to infinity. I offer you a seat at our right hand."

"You speak flowery words," Cassandra said. "But we have lived under the reign of one horrible ruler. Aligning with another does not suit us."

"I do not wish to rule you," Nox said. "I wish to set you free. I can bring you back into the fold of the universe and allow you to unleash your vengeance on the gods that forced you into this prison. I do not want your allegiance. I want to give you your freedom."

"And what do you expect from us in return?" Delilah asked.

"Loyalty. And patience," Nox replied. "The gods have done a good job locking up the beauty that we wished the universe to become, and all I ask is that you help us take it back. For that you will be rewarded with all the riches of all the galaxies, and power so great even the gods could not imagine it."

I had fallen in the thrall of pretty words like hers before. Had I not just told the others that I did not wish to rule; that what I wished was to find a quiet place on the Dark Planet and set up a small fiefdom? Was I really considering aligning myself with whatever Nox had become?

Lydia's voice echoed in my head. "Can you really release us from this prison?"

"Who do you think bound you here in the first place, among the shadows? The gods kept me from bringing you back when they locked the door, but now that it is open again, I can simply snap my fingers, and this planet will be restored to its rightful place."

Lydia glanced at me and the others. "I would like to eviscerate the gods that forced us to suffer here."

"And I would very much enjoy having the freedom to roam the universe, conquering whatever lands I choose," Delilah added.

Cassandra turned to me. "I don't...what do you think, Nimue? You are the only one of us who has been to the rest of the universe."

The moment of truth. Should I align myself with a malevolent force in the pursuit of more power, or go off among the shadows to live in peace? If I walked away, then I would assuredly be left to wallow in the new world order. It was better to align myself with power, even if I hated the idea, and then find a way to destroy it later.

"I have made deals with much worse to get much less than freedom. I do not know what she aims to do, but if the gods are her enemy, then the enemy of my enemy is my friend."

Nox smiled, studying me. "You are very wise, Nimue, and you will not regret this."

"I have learned it doesn't pay to regret anything."

CHAPTER 8
ROSE

I knew a final battle was coming with the Spore, but I didn't expect it so soon. I didn't think they'd find our well-hidden base or target Kadlu's shack with such ease and precision.

"They're leveling the city!" Chelle shouted as silt and dirt rained down from the ceiling. "Do you think they know we're underground?"

"If they don't know it won't take them long to figure it out," Kadlu replied.

The ceiling collapsed and from the dirt rose a figure with black eyes. Kadlu reached into her pocket and pulled out a handful of the blue spores we used to cure Rama. She blew them in the god's face, and he fell down.

"Let's go," Rama said. "He's not a threat anymore."

I looked up. Dozens of figures lit against the dark sky that poured rain onto the muddy ground. "We don't have enough to change them all."

"We can get more when we're off the planet," Rama said.

"If we get off the planet," Chelle corrected. "And we still

haven't figured out where to get it, if we do. This is hopeless an—"

"Don't think like that, baby." I squeezed her palm. "We're not going to let anything happen to you."

She looked away from the sky when the acid rain began to fall. "I believe that, Rose, but I don't think anyone can save me from those things."

"Well, we're sure as hell going to try."

The screams of other citizens filled the tunnels as we raced through. A half dozen of them were knocked back by a pair of blue haired gods.

"They're sitting ducks!" I shouted. "The gods will bury them when they find out we aren't there!"

Kadlu pulled me down an ancillary tunnel. "We can't worry about them now. If we don't stop the Spore and protect Chelle until we do, then nothing else is going to matter. If we want to save them, we have to save ourselves."

We needed more of the antidote—a lot more, given their numbers—but we had no idea where to find it. We had tried to visit the planet that Kadlu originally used to procure her antidote for Rama, except there was nothing but a planet charred to ash. She sent Maricel to scout another planet as we came up with another plan, but her sister hadn't come back yet, and we needed a solution now.

"How are we going to beat two dozen gods?" Chelle asked as the tunnels narrowed.

"We don't. We just get out of here as fast as possible. The Obsidian Spindle is our only option."

"With a force like that," I said. "They'll be able to destroy the universe."

"They have no interest in destroying the universe," Rama said. "Just the gods that control it. This is the perfect situation for them. They can use the same gods who oppressed them to save their brethren. I can't think of anything more ironic."

An explosion above us rocked the ceiling. Kadlu smashed through a thin wall in the cavern as the path ahead collapsed and prevented us from moving forward.

"Here!" she shouted.

There was no path forward for us once we reached the other side of the tunnel, just a small access door that she pushed open, and a ladder that led up beyond it. Rama took the lead and twisted open a port that led into a warehouse. When we were all safely up the ladder, Kadlu took a moment to catch her breath before standing up straight. "Is everyone okay?"

"Absolutely not," I said, covered in dirt. "But I'm not dead, so that's something."

"And I am dead," Chelle said. "But I guess I'm still alive, even though things would be much easier if I just died."

"Don't say that," I said, rubbing her arm. Dirt rose from her skin in clouds.

"Think about it," she replied. "If I just died, then the Spore couldn't use me to destroy the world."

"I'm not even sure you can die," Rama said, as if considering this. "But I must admit, that would put an end to this..."

"No!" I shouted. "We're not even going to entertain that option."

"Don't be stupid, Rose," Chelle said, taking both of my hands in hers. "Maybe it's the only way."

"I let you die to save the world once, Chelle. I'm not letting you do it again. Even you don't have that much of a savior complex."

Our moment didn't last long before an explosion ripped

the roof off the warehouse. A fierce goddess stared down at us.

"Athena," Chelle said. "This is bad."

"It's already pretty bad," I replied. "Not sure how much worse it could get."

"No," Kadlu said. "This is real, real bad."

CHAPTER 9

RED

No. Not again.

I had been tied up this way before, when Zabasha had attempted to destroy the Underworld. I yanked and pulled at the inky black goo that held me incapacitated in the air, but it was no use. I was helpless to watch as the creature controlling Nox made a deal with my greatest enemy. She promised not to interfere in my vengeance, and yet she'd held me back, bound so that I could not complete my task.

"There is just one final thing, Nimue, before we can cement our alliance."

"Of course there is," Nimue groaned. "There always is. And what is that?"

Nox snapped her fingers and my chains disappeared. I caught myself before smashing my face into the ground, then jumped up and pulled out my daggers.

"I'll kill you!" I roared.

I didn't know whether my angry words were directed to Nox, Nimue, or both, but my feet directed me toward Nox, and I swiped at her with a pair of daggers. She didn't move, except to press her hand into my chest and send a shock-wave through me.

"This woman is very important to me," Nox said to Nimue. "And she has quite a grudge against you. I promised she would have a chance to vindicate herself before I killed her."

Kill me? Was that why she was being so kind to me? Was Nox leading me like a lamb to slaughter?

"That's rich. Do you still think of me, Red?" Nimue said, cracking a smile. "That is the greatest pain I could inflict on you, and it brings me great joy to be so deep inside your head."

I held up my dagger. "I will dig this deep into your head to return the favor."

Nox laughed. "This is quite unorthodox, but I thought you could kill two birds with one stone, as the saying goes." She turned to Nimue. "If you can defeat Gabrielle, then you have my allegiance in the new world order."

"And if she can't?" Cassandra said.

"Then she will be dead, and this will all sort itself out. I will warn you, though, that you cannot kill my pet without terrible consequences."

"But she can kill me?" Nimue said.

A wicked, unnatural smile spread across Nox's face. "I didn't say it would be a fair fight. You have magic, after all, and she just has two small daggers. This should be a piece of cake for you."

I had hoped to sneak up on Nimue from the shadows, not come at her head on, but I had to admit that Nox had fulfilled her promise to let me get my revenge. I would not squander it.

"We won't let her hurt you, sister," Delilah said.

"No." Nox held up her hand. "This is Nimue's fight, and

hers alone. If you interfere, I will see to it your fate is the same as your sister."

She pointed to Baba's dead body, headless and weeping black bile onto the ground. Delilah spat on it.

"She is no sister of ours. Good riddance she is dead."

"However you feel about her," Nox said. "I am very sure you do not want to end up like her. Stay out of the fray. There will be no warnings, only consequences."

"Your new visage suits you, Nimue," I said. "Now your insides match your outsides; hideous and warped."

"We have not fought in a long time, Red. I have learned much since our time in the Dream Realm, whereas it seems like you have lost a step and are showing every bit of your age."

I leapt to attack before she could respond. She dodged my attack with an elegant spin and a speed I didn't think possible given the smoothness of her movements. Five crackles of lightning shot from her fingers. I rolled forward to avoid them, replacing my attack dagger with three throwing ones as I did so. When I rose again, I tossed them into the black space where her heart once stood.

She simply smiled. "Once, that would have dusted me. Now, I am more powerful than even Hypnos himself." With a single clap of her hands, a fissure opened under me. A dozen black hands rose from it, trying to pull me down to them. I leapt to avoid them, slicing at one as it wrapped around my ankle.

In my quest for revenge, I hadn't considered Nimue becoming more powerful. Now, I worried that my hatred would not be enough to kill her. I needed my golden dagger. It was enough to fell even a god, but I left it with Chelle so she could protect herself. I only hoped that if I died this day, she would have made use of it. I glanced around me for an opening. The eyes of the princesses were glued to me. Perhaps I could escape and lick my wounds if I caused a big enough distraction...or if I played on Nimue's legendary temper to do the work for me.

"You have certainly learned some nice parlor tricks," I said. "But Hypnos would wipe the floor with you."

"No god can touch me!" Nimue shrieked. A wave of fire shot from her.

I flung a half dozen more daggers at her as I ducked the blast of fire. "Do you have a power complex, Nimue? It's okay to admit you are a weak child."

"Nobody calls me weak!"

This time a great blast of force shot through the room, unmooring me, and the ground cracked along with it. The assembled crowd fell to their knees. One more sloppy attack like that would distract the others, which would give me an opportunity to flee into the town below.

I backed up. "Queen Aine knew the truth, even all those years ago. That you are a coward who could only rule through fear, and even in that, you fail."

"You insolent cur," she shouted, her alabaster skin quite a bit redder than just moments ago.

The whole top of the hill began to shake, and that time, even Nox fell to her knees.

"Watch yourself," the goddess warned, taking her eyes off me to steady herself.

I took the opportunity to rush to the edge of the cliff and leap, knowing whatever I found in the town below would be friendlier than the monsters that ruled it, and if not, I would far rather take my chances with them.

CHAPTER 10

CHELLE

When she'd come to see me in Odin's prison, Red gave me a golden dagger that she promised could kill a god. I waited until Frigg came to feed me and used it on her. She thought I was powerless, but I showed her. Then I took that same dagger and plunged it into Odin's back, saving Rose. It wasn't enough, not nearly enough, but it was my little part to play in her escaping the Spore.

My hand was on the hilt of that dagger again now, before Athena even lowered herself to the ground.

"We do not wish to destroy this planet," she said. Her voice was stilted and wooden. So unlike the god who stole me from Earth to begin this whole affair. "Give us the girl and we will spare the rest of you."

"The gods condemned this place already. There is no saving it." Kadlu laughed. "You made a big mistake turning Athena. There are plenty of gods I would fight to save, but Athena is one I would kill even if she wasn't one of you."

Athena cocked her head. "You survived us once. It is a mistake that we will not abide a second time."

Athena unsheathed a great sword that pulsated with

blue energy. Set against her black eyes and the darkness of the room, it cast a haunting image. Kadlu reached into her pocket and withdrew out a small baton. She pulled on the edges to expand it to a bow, which she twirled in her hands.

"Get them out of here, Rama," Kadlu said, not taking her eyes off of Athena. "The Spore are an interconnected brain, which means that the others will be here soon enough."

"I'm not leaving you," he replied.

She whirled to face him. "I never thought I would see you again. That we had these days together has meant everything, even if we never have another one." She smirked. "However, if you think I'm going to lose to Athena, you must be out of your mind."

The goddess rushed forward and swung her sword, but Kadlu slid under her legs and smashed her in the back of the head.

"Go!" Kadlu shouted.

I gave her one last look before rushing out of the door with Rose and Rama. As we did, two more gods smashed through the ceiling. There was a glint of fear in Kadlu's eyes, but she didn't let it stop her. She simply mouthed "Go," and I rushed out the door. If she died, I would not let her sacrifice be in vain.

The rain burned my skin, but I gritted through the pain. "Follow me," I said, speeding to the front of the pack. I led Rose and Rama toward the next building and used it as cover, then exited out the back. Through the heavy rain, I could make out two figures approaching us through the mud. I grabbed the hilt of my dagger tighter and slid out toward the one on the left. Before it had a chance to attack, I buried the blade deep into its chest.

I would only get one surprise attack, because now all

the Spore knew where we were. The other god rushed toward us. I went to attack when Rose screamed, and a hundred shards of ice punctured the god sending it flying backwards. It wasn't enough to kill it, but her spell gave me the jump on him, and I leapt to plunge the dagger into its throat.

"We make a good team," I said, grinning. The acid had burned against her skin, and it had already started to scab. I kissed her, hard.

"I already knew that," she said with a smile when I finally let go of her.

"This is a touching moment and all," Rama said. "But can we keep going before the gods come after us?"

"Right," I said. I winked at Rose. "To be continued."

CHAPTER 11
NIMUE

"What have you done?" Nox shouted as she watched Red disappear down the cliff that dropped precipitously from where the rose garden used to be, and where I once held a brief conversation with Rapunzel who had masked herself in the thatch.

"Seems like she got away," Delilah said. "A pity."

"A pity?" Nox wheeled on her. "That is all you have to say, that this is a pity? Do you have any idea what you have done?"

I held up my hands. "First of all, you told me to fight that girl. If you had asked me, I would have told you she was one of the trickiest people I have ever had the displeasure of knowing, and one of the most cowardly as well."

"Are you raising your voice?" Nox growled.

This was not my first time in the presence of a dictator. I had just destroyed one, and I recognized one when they were in front of me. Nox didn't even wear a good disguise.

"I am." I leveled my gaze at her. "You told me that you offered freedom, and freedom means the ability to tell people they are idiots, and you are being an idiot. However,

I suspect what you want is to subjugate us like everyone else."

Nox's face twisted in fury. The minute you found the truth about a power-mad dictator, their true face revealed itself, and hers was ugly. "How dare you!"

"You sound like a broken record," I said. "Now, leave. Or I will be forced to make you leave."

"We will be forced to make you leave," Delilah added, stepping forward. Her hands glowed a haunting green, like what you would find burning a cursed object in a dark dungeon.

"Enough talk," Lydia growled into our brains. "Cover your eyes!"

She raised her hand and the entire sky turned white. I felt the heat of a sun shining down on us and closed my eyes just as a cooling wind blew through. A second later it was over, and when I opened my eyes, Nox was screaming bloody murder, her eyes a milky white instead of the dead black they had been moments before.

"What have you done?" she screamed, flailing her arms wildly. "I can't see!"

Delilah opened her mouth and let out a scream. It cut through my body, and I shivered, but it quickly dissipated, at least for me. It must have caught Nox fully because she grabbed her ears and fell to the ground.

Before Nox could stand up again, Delilah muttered a spell that created a half dozen copies of herself. All of them attacked at once, slicing Nox with pieces of glass from the wreckage, leaving them embedded in her chest.

"Enough!" Nox shouted, staggering to her feet. "I grow tired of this. Find the girl and deliver her to the Oracle at the center of Celestial Realm by tomorrow or I will return with a hundred gods and raze this realm to the ground. The door I entered through in the far woods that have no canopy will lead you to my lair."

In a flash, she teleported herself forward and snatched up pieces of Rapunzel's body before disappearing once again, leaving behind the stench of her burning flesh.

"We should go after her!" Cassandra said. "I didn't even get a chance to fight!"

"No," I said. "I'm sure she's gone from this place now. She is too much of a coward to risk another fight with us at our full power. The best we can do now is find Gabrielle."

The princesses looked at each other, confused. We had just defeated a god, and we had victory pulsating through our veins, but it was a false confidence. We had dealt a blow to Nox, and she knew we were formidable now.

"You don't aim to do what she says, do you?" Delilah asked.

"No," I replied. "But if she has use of Red, then we have use of her, too, as a bargaining chip if nothing else. After all, the enemy of my enemy is my friend, right?"

"And what if they are both your enemy?" Cassandra asked.

Red had always been an antagonist to me, but perhaps she was not the enemy I always believed her to be. She was a survivor, of course, but her moral compass always pointed to justice. If I could show her that the only true justice lied in destroying Nox, then perhaps I could get her on my side, for a time at least. If she survived the final battle, then I would deal with her then. You did not keep a thorn in your side for long, even if it was a useful thorn.

Besides, what better way to shame your enemy than to convince them to do your bidding. That was true power.

"Then we pit them against each other and stand back to rule over the rubble."

CHAPTER 12

CHELLE

I wasn't a murderer, but I was a killer. All the way back to Earth, when people came after me for being a gorgon, I dealt with them. Sometimes, that meant roughing them up, other times it meant sending a message, but if they came after me and wouldn't let up, sometimes they left me no choice. I regretted the first few because I'm not a monster no matter what people think, but after a while, the pain of killing was replaced with a hollowness. It carves a piece out of you to kill, even if it's self-defense. It puts you in a horrible club; the kind of club you never want to enter.

When I was young, my mother tried to prepare me for it as best she could. She had been alive a long time and knew that humanity would never accept us. After monsters were outed on Earth and people had no choice but to accept them, I thought maybe that would be the end of my hiding; the end of my endless need to kill to protect myself and my family. I was never so naïve as to truly believe it, but I hoped, even if it was a fool's hope. When the protests started, I knew my mother's greatest fears were true. Humanity would never accept us.

"Are you okay?" Rose asked as I stared down at the golden dagger. We'd finally stopped to rest.

"I'm fine." I wiped the remaining blood off the dagger. "It had to be done."

"You're right," Rama said, looking out the door to find the next safe spot. The gods were tracking us across the city, fanning out to search every building they hadn't destroyed. "They're getting close."

"Maybe we can go back down into the tunnels," Rose said.

Rama turned to us. "We'll be caged down there, like mole rats. They could just collapse the tunnels if they found us inside and bury us alive. We would be helpless." He looked down at the sores on his arms from the burning acid rain. "This is more painful, but at least here we have a chance."

He beckoned us forward, and we moved between the buildings to the next one a hundred feet away. As we did, I heard the crackling of gunfire through the pouring rain.

"What are they doing?"

Rama smiled as we pushed open the doors. "People on this planet hate the gods. They have been waiting for this day for years, decades even, waiting for a chance to take revenge for their ancestors."

"They're fighting the gods?" Rose asked. "They're going to die."

"They're going to die anyway," Rama said. "At least this way they go out in a blaze of glory."

"That's crazy," I said as we climbed to the second floor of the building. "I love it."

"Look," Rama said, pointing to the window.

I stared out the window as a pack of gods entered one side of the square. As they did, the buildings across the square lit up with machine gun fire before a pair of rockets fired on the gods. The militia wasn't able to slow them down, but they were at least a distraction.

"Maybe that will give us some cover."

We rushed back down the stairs and out the back. The pounding of the rain matched the blistering pace of my heart as I thought about the militia's futile attack. They would all die in a matter of moments, but they weren't fighting for themselves. They were fighting for their ancestors; for the generations upon generations that were screwed over by the gods.

I felt a kinship to those militia members. Athena once told me she created my kind as a way for us to fight back against our oppressors and never be the victim again, but we had been a victim every day since, picked out for being different, and hunted for being misunderstood. All because of a god's whim.

I did not want the Primordials to return, and I did not want to be killed to do so, but part of me understood the Spore, and in another life, we might have even fought on the same side.

Not in this life though, and the next one wasn't looking good either.

CHAPTER 13
ARIEL

Urgu was black, gray, and filled with fire. I pushed myself up from the cobblestones and watched the denizens of the Emerald City scream as they ran past, pushing their way through the crowd. An amorphous blob with bright orange eyes rolled down the street, gobbling up everything in its path, including people.

I spun on my heels and started sprinting away. I leapt over a woman who had been thrown to the ground, and an instant later my heart called out to her. Against all better judgement, I turned and ran through the sea of people back to her.

"Can you move?" I asked.

"I think so."

Sprained ankles weren't something that souls could technically get, but the mind was a powerful beast and could trick you into just about anything, including the fact that you were still alive, even if you'd been lost in the Dream Realm for a hundred years.

I pulled the woman to her feet as the blob loomed over us. She hobbled along, and I threw her arm over my shoulder to help her keep pace with me. However, within a couple feet it was clear that the blob was gaining on us.

"Leave me," she said, wincing. She tried to pull herself away from me.

I held my grasp tighter, looking for any way to escape. There was a brownstone next to us, its door green and festooned with a wreath. I kicked at the knob until it snapped off. Then, I rammed my shoulder into the door and shoved the woman inside before diving in after her. I wedged the door back into place just as the ooze of the blob seeped inside.

"Get that table!" I shouted, pointing to the dining room table on the far side of the room. The woman limped over as fast as she could, then slid the table toward me, leaving scratches along the floor.

We shoved the table in front of the door, then added a couch and two end tables. The blob flowed inside. I thought we would be safe for a moment, but in the kitchen, the ooze was dripping down through the flue.

"This is not good," the woman said, looking up. The ceiling creaked.

A second later, the wood above us snapped and the ooze flooded the living room. Its horrible odor made me want to wretch. We scrambled to a bedroom at the end of the hall. The ceiling above was thick with rot and I knew we wouldn't be safe for long.

"Go," I shouted, yanking the window open.

The woman hesitated, and I shoved her through the small opening into the courtyard. I went to join her when she screamed out in fear. The blob dripped down and swallowed her whole, turning her into dust. I rushed across the hallway into an office.

"*Terrae motus*," I said, laying my hands on the wall.

It quaked and sheared, a hole ripped in it big enough to jump through, which I did. The next room was buckling with the weight of the blob, and I sped through just as the room caved in.

"*Augue!*" I shouted when I reached the other side of the townhouse, and a fireball shot from my fingers, causing a chain reaction that collapsed the walls.

I nearly made it through, covered in dust and debris, before the ooze dripped upon my shoulder. It ate through my shirt in an instant and burned my flesh. I couldn't imagine what more than a drop would do, as even the smallest amount was enough to rip a chunk out of my soul and turn it to dust.

"*Celeritas!*" I yelled, laying hands on myself, and this time I rushed through the house with more speed, blasting through the next wall before the blob had a chance to reach it. When I reached the street again, the blob was bigger and even more powerful.

"Attack," a small but mighty voice cried, and a squad of fairies flew forward, throwing magical attacks at the blob. That seemed to slow it down, and every explosion from their tiny, powerful hands blew bits of it away.

I didn't wait to see whether the blob could be defeated. I sprinted toward the castle. From there, I could get to the sea, but something told me that the whole of Urgu was under attack. When the Nightmare Realm attacked last time, the sea was the only place that remained untouched by the destruction. I hoped that was true this time as well. Otherwise, they might have found the sword, and this would have all been for naught.

CHAPTER 14

ROSE

Moving through the city was slow and plodding with the constant attacks from the gods high above and the acid rain that burned us every time we stepped out into the open. Not to mention the militia attacking the gods every chance it got. However, after hours of maneuvering, we finally came to the edge of the city.

"Wait here," Rama said, waving the shotgun he'd pulled from an empty building. His arms and face were badly burned. Chelle and I were no better, and even the snakes on her head were raw with damage. "I need a minute."

"Probably best to catch our breath while the rain dies down," Chelle said. "Climbing the mountain is going to take the rest of our energy if we aren't careful."

It was a double-edged sword. The rain gave us cover from the gods, but it also made it so that our bodies were rubbed raw by staying out in it for too long.

"Let me see," I said, moving toward her.

There was a small gas lamp in the tin shack that hid us from the gods and the elements. I brought her over to it and ran my hands over the snakes on her head.

"*Sana*," I whispered.

My hands glowed a light yellow as I rubbed Albie's head. At first, he hissed at me and pulled back, but when he realized I was trying to heal him and that my touch could heal his blistered skin, he allowed me to pet him. As his skin returned to a dark green, the other snakes begged for my help. I healed them all as best I could.

I was not a healer by trade, but then I wasn't supposed to have magic at all. It was only by the grace of two gods I could wield anything that would help anyone. Now, I was being asked to turn against the very beings that gave me that power if I wanted to save the universe.

"That feels nice," Chelle said as the snakes on her head healed.

It had never been clear to me whether the snakes were a part of Chelle or their own entities, but one thing I knew was that when they hurt, she hurt as well, and vice versa. Death had made them cagey, and torture had made them wary, but they still yearned for my touch when they were fully healed, just as Chelle did.

I traced my fingers from the snakes down to Chelle's cheeks. They had been badly burned by the acid, and my touch brought them back to their dark mocha coloring.

"You should save some of that for yourself," she said. "You look terrible."

I smiled. "I don't have to look at myself. I have to look at you, though, and seeing you in pain bums me out."

"So, this is all about you, then?" she said with a smile. "Figures."

"Of course," I replied. "You know how selfish I am."

Chelle laughed. "That's the funniest thing you have ever said. If you were selfish, then we would be on a beach somewhere, on a long-forgotten planet, living in blissful ignorance of the plight of the universe."

I looked away. "I don't think that's true. I think it would have come to us. The only way to get peace is to finish this, and that is just about as selfish as it gets."

She wrapped her raw hands around mine, and they began to heal. "No matter whether you think it's selfish or not, you are still sacrificing yourself to better the universe, and that is noble."

"I am sacrificing myself to save you. I once chose the universe over you and look where that got us." I choked on my words. "And you choosing to save the Dream Realm over us made you a cog in this stupid machine of death, whatever it is. Being heroes has brought us nothing but pain."

"It hasn't been all bad. It also made you the queen of Oz, and a powerful wielder of magic."

"I would give it all back if we could just go back to blissful ignorance."

"I don't think you would, not really. Gun to your head, would you really rather be at home, not knowing the world was about to end, or fighting to do something about it?"

I was sure I knew the answer to that question, and yet I couldn't get myself to say it. "I don't know. What I do know is that I miss Cheyenne, and I miss our bed."

"I miss her, too, but if you didn't save the Fairy Realm, we never would have been in New York, and we never would have gotten her. So, like I said, it hasn't been all bad."

"I'm not used to you being the positive one. It's weird, but I think I like it." My face turned down. I thought about our little dog often, and whether Jamil was taking advantage of my credit card to give her all the amenities that I never did. "Do you think Cheyenne will remember us, if we get home?"

"When you get home, she'll be glued to you for days."

"When we get home, you mean."

"I can be positive for you, my love, but it's hard to see me getting out of this one, when the pantheon is out to make sure I die."

"We've survived worse."

"No, we haven't."

"No," I replied with a small smile. "But we will. We always have."

"You always have. I already died once." She sighed. "I just hope that if it happens again, then it's for good this time. Take me out of this universe, dust me into oblivion. This is all too much bullshit, and it never ends."

"Hey!" I shouted. "Don't say that. We have a plan to meet at Persephone's palace, remember? We're going to spend eternity together. Don't you forget that."

"I know, but I feel like that guy at the end of *The Green Mile*. 'I'm tired, boss. I'm so tired of this shit.'"

I squeezed her hand. "Tough. You don't get rid of me that easily. I'll be annoying you in death just like I do in life."

"You're not annoying." She touched her forehead to mine. "You're the only good thing in this universe, Rose. No matter what happens, I want you to remember that."

I'm not sure how long we stayed like that, eyes closed, listening to each other breathe, but eventually Rama tapped my shoulder.

"Sorry to interrupt, lovebirds, but it looks like there's a break in the patrol. We should go now."

I sighed. "Time to save the universe, I guess."

"And then we can rest, right?" Chelle asked, pulling away.

"And then we can rest."

CHAPTER 15

RED

Don't freak out, Gabrielle. I just happened to be in a bizarre world with my nemesis chasing me—at the behest of a god that had been taken over by a malevolent entity that wanted to destroy the universe.

No problem whatsoever.

"Are you from the castle?" a soft voice asked.

I was hiding behind a wooden barrel. Peeking around its side was a purple girl with black eyes and four tentacles sticking out of the top of her head. She cradled something fluffy with six arms that wrapped around her body.

"No—" I decided not to couch my words, despite the danger. "I mean, I did escape from there, but I'm not from there."

"Do you know what happened up there?" Her eyes were wide.

I pursed my lips. "I'm not sure, but it looked like there was a great battle."

"Do you know what happened to the King in Yellow?"

I thought for a moment. "There was a skeleton covered in a yellow cape. It looked dead. Maybe that was him."

Her eyes lit up and she ran off, calling, "Mommy!"

If she told her mother where I was, I didn't know what would happen. I chased the child into a house at the end of the street. Inside, a woman that looked like a bigger version of the girl turned from washing dishes, her apron covered in muck and grime.

"What are you hollering about litt—" She froze when she saw me. "Who are you?"

"She's from the castle!" the girl screamed.

The mother held up all her arms in a defensive position, half across her own body and half across her daughter's. "We want no quarrel with you. We've paid up our taxes, and if my girl said anything to offend you, she's very sorry. Please don't take her away from me."

"I..." My brows furrowed. "I'm not here to hurt you or take your daughter away. I'm fleeing Nimue and the other —" I'd said too much. I didn't know this woman's allegiances, so I simply knelt on the ground. "I'm sorry for scaring you. I'll be going now."

"Mommy!" The girl pulled on her mother's apron. "She said Hastur is dead!"

"Don't say that name!" The mother clapped her daughter's mouth closed and scanned the room. When nothing happened, she relaxed. "You aren't lying, are you, stranger?"

I shook my head. "In truth, I do not know the fate of the one you speak about. I simply told the girl what I knew— that I saw the body—and she inferred from there."

"Uttering the king's name is a punishable offense and yet, we are safe. What you say must be true." She walked forward and extended her hand to me. "Stand, stranger. You look weary. Can I offer you a bed to rest in?"

"Thank you." I took her hand and stood. "But what I really need is a way out of this city without being detected. I need to travel to a forest with no leaves, where the branches form a canopy over everything."

She thought for a moment. "I do not know of such a place, but I can bring you to one who is more traveled than any I have met in my life. If any can help you, it is them."

"Thank you. I would be most appreciative of your help."

She slid forward. "You have brought glad tidings, stranger. It is the least I can do." She broke off her words and stared at the ceiling at the sounds of feet scurrying across it. Her daughter suddenly did the same. "You need to hide."

I didn't ask any questions. She opened a cabinet under her stove and shoved me inside, closing it tight behind her.

"You spoke the word," a voice whispered. I recognized it from the mountain but didn't dare open the cabinet to see. I deduced she was one of Nimue's cronies.

"My daughter did, great Delilah. Please, she did not mean it."

The voice growled. "That is not my concern now. I seek a human woman that looks like none you will have seen in your life. She is not ashen like those you know, but has skin of peach, along with bright green eyes, and a long red cape."

"Sounds horrible," the girl said. "Humans are gross."

"Amnita," the mother said. "That's not nice."

"Have you seen this woman?" the woman they called Delilah asked.

There was a long silence, followed by a sigh, when I was sure I was defeated. "I'm sorry to say I haven't. Is everything alright?"

The monster's stoic nature emboldened me. I wasn't used to people standing up to power.

"No, nothing is alright, and it won't be until we find that woman," Delilah said. "If you see her, only say the word and I will return." There was a long pause. "And if I find you are lying...well, I don't have to remind you what I did to your husband. I would hate for the same fate to come to your daughter."

"Please, don't touch my daughter," the mother sniffled. "I'm sorry, but—we have not seen this woman. If we do, I swear by the dark king that I will say the word."

"See that you do."

There was a pop and then the woman let out a breath of air. After several more seconds passed, she came over to the cabinet and opened the door. "I don't know what you have done to piss off the princesses, but anyone who can irritate them so is okay in my book."

"Are those the women I saw at the castle?" When the monster nodded her gelatinous form, I continued. "You do not like the princesses?"

"We hate them," the girl yelled. "Daddy fought against them...and then they killed him."

"That's enough, Amnita. But it is true. My Nyrorpip tried until his last breath to get the dark king off the throne."

"I am glad to know you, then. Any enemy of my enemy is a friend of mine."

"Come," she said, putting on a bonnet. "Let us make you look the part, and then I will take you to see my cousin."

"A thousand thank yous," I replied.

"Don't thank me yet. The road will be filled with perils, and my cousin is no great joy, either."

"Whatever the risk, it will be worth it after what I have been through in the past few months."

"If that is true, then I truly pity you."

CHAPTER 16
ARIEL

The streets were nearly empty as the spires of the castle came into view, but the air was still tense with fear. The closer I came to the castle, the more that tension grew, until I rounded the corner to see the citizens of the Emerald City locked in battle with the guards against the monsters of the Nightmare Realm. The guards were losing, badly. The castle was in serious danger of being overrun by the horrors of the great abyss at any moment.

"Ariel?" The voice was familiar.

Canterbury, the mutated rabbit from the Nightmare Realm, was covered in the ash of fallen souls, staring at me. "My gods, look at you. One day outside of Sprig and you turned back into a savage."

"What?" He looked down at his body. "Oh, this. No, you got it all wrong. I didn't kill anybody—I'm not even in this fight—but when you're in the midst of a battle, you get a bit dirty."

"If you're not fighting, why are you here?"

"I'm looking for Kelvin and the others you brought back from the Nightmare Realm. You told me you were taking them to the Emerald City, so I thought I would come and try to protect them."

"Oh," my eyes turned down. Tears welled in my eyes. "Then you don't know—"

"Know what?" His eyes went wide. "Oh no."

"Nox...she met us at the portal, and"—I started to cry heavily—"she slaughtered them all. I'm so sorry. I told you I was going to protect them, and I led them to their deaths."

Canterbury choked back his emotions. "Nox...she's the one who tore open the portals to the Dream Realm. She tore holes all over the realm. I didn't know...I thought..." He looked up at me, venom in his eyes. "You were supposed to protect them!"

"I know," I replied. "I'm so sorry. She ambushed us, and she took me prisoner. I'm not even here, not really. My body is somewhere else, tied up, waiting to die. I need to get to the sea and find something called the Hope Bringer sword so that I can fix this before my body dies in the real world and I'm stuck—well, I don't even know if I would come back here if I died. It's all very confusing."

Canterbury bit his lip. "Kelvin just wanted to get here. He said everything would be okay if he could just get to the Dream Realm, and look what happened. He got here and it killed him." Determination rose on his face. "I'll help you get to the sea. Not for you, but for Kelvin."

"Why would you do that?"

"Kelvin told me a lot about what this place was like. He dreamed about it every day, and now...it's nothing like what he imagined. If you can make this place like his dream, then at least in some small way, maybe he won't be completely dead. But make no mistake, once this is over, I want nothing to do with you. I will never forgive you."

"Thank you, but I don't know how we will get through these monsters."

"Leave that to me."

He tapped on his chest three times, and the great Seeker who had chased me all over the Nightmare Realm burst from it, rising until it was a dozen feet tall, all arms and legs stretched like a shadow in the early morning sun.

"We need to get out of the city," Canterbury said to the monster, who nodded. "Don't fight this time, okay?"

The Seeker's long arms dragged on the ground and scooped me up into its arms. Its hands were big enough to close around me, giving me nothing but a small hole to see out of into the wreckage of the Emerald City.

With its other arm, the Seeker grabbed Canterbury and placed him on its shoulder. It loped away from the battle and towards the edge of the city, toward my destiny, and the salvation of Urgu.

The rain had died down, but the acid water still sloshed against my legs and feet as we moved toward the mountain that housed the Obsidian Spindle. My shoes had been eaten through and the water burned my feet, but I swallowed my pain, as I saw the ache also on Rama's face, and Rose's. She had taken the time to heal us before the final ascent to the Spindle, but it didn't take long before we were covered in acid marks again.

"It looks like the coast is cle—"

A massive fireball exploded in front of him, sending him flying backward. Rose rushed to his side immediately, and I looked back to see a half dozen gods flying toward us.

"*Sana*," she whispered. "*Sana!*" She turned to me. "It's not working."

"The gods..." Rama croaked. "Their magic is more powerful than yours. If they want you to suffer, then you will, and they want me to suffer."

"I don't believe that!" Rose screamed. "*Sana! Sana! Sana!*"

I placed my hand on her shoulder. "We have to go. Now."

"No!" Rose screamed.

Rama grabbed her hand. "She's right. The place—the place I wanted to bring you. Elvirion. We used to—it was the place I grew up. The Spore had no use for my memories before I became a god. Go there. It is...paradise."

With that, he fell to the ground as he expelled his last breath, and his eyes grew glassy. Rose started to cry immediately.

"No, it's not—No. Come back. Come back!"

I pulled her away. "It's okay, Rose. It's okay. If he's a human, we'll see him again in the Underworld. He's not gone. He's just moved on."

She buried her face in my shoulder, sobbing. "It's not fair. It's not fair."

My shirt was damp with her tears. "None of this is fair."

A fireball hurtled toward us. I threw up a forcefield around us that blocked it but still we were sent flying backward from the impact. I wrapped my hands around Rose and held her tight as my back slammed into the ground.

Rose pushed herself up from the ground and turned to the gods. One of her eyes had turned pink and the other red. She clapped her hands together and a shockwave shot across the ground, knocking the gods out of the air. Next, she pulled down a lightning strike that shocked their writhing bodies. Before they had stopped sizzling, she called forth a dozen demon dogs from the bowels of Hell.

"Kill them," she said, quietly and composed.

The dogs began to rip the gods apart. They kicked and screamed to avoid being eaten alive. Rose closed her eyes, and the ground in front of us turned to lava, pulling the gods down into the ground, and then she covered them with the earth.

"What are you doing?"

"Coming into my power."

The gods smashed upward through the ground and rose into the air. When they did, Rose twirled her hands around and called forth a tornado. As they struggled to escape Rose threw huge boulders at them. When it was over, the gods laid on the ground.

"Give me the dagger." She held her hand out. When I hesitated, she turned to me, her eyes aglow. "Now."

"You don't want to do this," I said. "I'll do it."

She didn't wait for me. She reached forward and pulled the golden dagger from my hand like I was a child withholding a toy. She marched forward, using her power to smash the gods again and again into the ground.

I followed behind, pleading with her to stop, but she had gone feral. When she reached the gods, she held them in the air. One by one, she stabbed them through the heart, until only one remained.

When she spoke, her voice was low and dark. It sent a chill up my spine. "You are Spore, so I hope you understand what I have done to your people. I am done playing around. Leave us alone, or you will feel my full wrath. If I have to kill every one of you myself, I will, and I will enjoy the privilege. Take the Celestial Realm. Have your revenge on the gods there but leave the Dream Realm alone. Leave the Underworld alone. Leave the Fairy Realm alone. Leave my friends alone, or you will see the full power of a woman scorned."

"We cannot." The final god smiled. "The Dream Realm will fall. They will all fall to us. And then the universe will be destroyed, only to be reborn again in our image."

Rose took a breath. "I hoped you would be more rational." She stabbed the god through the heart. "I suppose this means war, then."

When it was over, she fell to the ground, and I dropped next to her. She was weeping now, and her eyes were back to their normal blue. She looked down at her hands. "Did I really do all that?"

"Yeah," I replied. "It was completely badass."

"They were innocent. It's the Spore that—"

"They were not innocent. They might be under the control of the Spore, but no god is innocent, not even Hypnos."

I tried to be kind but underneath my support, I was scared for her, for us, and for everyone. Rose dropped the golden dagger, and it fell into my hands, covered in sticky blood from tip to hilt. "We should go, Rose. We'll have time to mourn the dead later."

She sniffled, nodding. "You're right. I know, you're right, but my legs refuse to move right now."

"Then I'll carry you."

CHAPTER 18

RED

The city under the destroyed castle in Carcosa was odd and filled with monsters of all types, from giants with orange fur to ones that were little more than an eyeball with legs and arms, but I was surprised by how similar it was to the world I knew. There were armorers and blacksmiths and fruit vendors (though with types of food I had never seen before, nor ever wanted to) and grocers, and just about any type of thing I would have found in the Dream Realm, all run by monsters instead of humans.

The only true monsters I had ever seen were from the Nightmare Realm, and they were mindless killers who had no sense of community. However, I recognized some of those same types of monsters oozing and walking their way through the cities like it was normal. There were humans in the mix, too, interacting with monsters like old friends. They were frail, with skin hanging off bone, but they were clearly human, and the monsters made no violence against them.

"This way," my new monster friend said, waving three of her arms toward a small shop sandwiched between a newspaper stand and a trinket shop. She had told me on our walk that her name was Yriz, and that she had lived in the city of Carcosa for her whole life, save for one summer when she traveled to the North when she was barely older than her daughter.

Yriz covered my face with soot and drew the mammoth hood over my face so that I could barely see where I was going. It was similar to my normal garb, except baggier, and she'd used an old brown cloak to cover my iconic red cape that made me stand out from the crowd.

"The humans of Carcosa are servants to the king," she told me. "They are not fed as well as you, and your plump face will stand out."

I found it best not to argue with locals, and simply followed what she told me as we shuffled through the city. She stopped in front of the darkened shop and knocked three times. "Virtrund, it's me, Yriz. Let me in."

After a short wait a small peephole slid open, and several eyes looked out at us. "You shouldn't have come here. The city is in disarray."

"I know." She beckoned me forward and pulled off my hood. "I have the one they are looking for."

"Hayseed!" Virtrund shouted. He opened the door and pulled us inside with what seemed like an infinite number of arms. When the door closed, several small purple flames sprang to life around the shop. "I don't want to be involved in this."

The shop wasn't much of one. Instead, it was a stock-pile of all sorts of weapons, armor, canned food, and other accoutrements that would usually be seen with a doomsday prepper back on Rose's Earth.

"You were once part of this rebellion just like Nyrorpip, and—"

"Don't use his name to curry favor with me. I know my past!" Virtrund snapped. "But his death sobered me up. I want nothing to do with that life."

"The king is dead," I said during the silence that followed his words. "You have nothing to fear from him anymore."

"You are not from here, or you would never address me with that much confidence." His thousand eyes all locked in on me. "What would you know about Carcosa, stranger? Have you seen the evil of the princesses? Do you know what they are capable of, even if the king is dead? He was horrible, but at least he brought stability. Now, everything will fracture, and the power hungry will come out to fight for the throne."

"It seemed like Nimue had it under control. I certainly wouldn't want to fight them," I said.

Virtrund chuckled. "You think Carcosa, let alone the whole of this planet, will kneel before women. You have another thing coming."

I stood straighter. "I do not claim to know your customs, but I think people will bow to whoever holds the power, and I have not seen any more powerful than Nimue."

"This is inconsequential, Virtrund!" Yriz growled. "I don't need you to risk your life. I simply need a way to get this woman out of the city and to—I'm sorry, where do you need to go?"

"A forest where the trees have no leaves, and the branches have fused together to create a canopy of—"

"Shariza," Virtrund said, looking me up and down. "They have opened the gate, then."

"What are you talking about?" Yriz asked.

"There has been a prophesy for as long as I could

remember that someday strangers and gods from a strange land would open the gate back to the universe and allow us access to it through the gate at the center of Shariza."

"You mean…we can leave this planet?" Yriz asked, a quiver in her voice.

"I don't know," Virtrund said, looking at me. "Can we?"

I thought for a moment. "I'm not sure if the door is still open, but I came through a gate built on another planet to be here, and if the name of the forest where the portal spat me out is Shariza, then I suppose yes, you can go through it. But only if it is still open."

"Once the gate opens, it cannot be closed so easily, according to legend." Virtrund turned to Yriz, excitement filled his voice. "If what she says is true, this changes every-thing. I must tell the others—"

"I need to go this instant," I said. "Please. The fate of the universe is at stake, not to mention my life."

"I will tell the others," Yriz said, shooing me forward. "If you have any love left for me, please take her to the forest."

Virtrund nodded. "Of course. I will bring you to Chil-drum on my way to—" His voice cracked. "This is all very exciting. You have no idea how long we have waited for a chance to leave this place."

"No, I don't," I replied. "But I have been a pilgrim in search of a way out of a distant land before, so I can under-stand your joy all too well."

CHAPTER 19

ROSE

"You can put me down now," I whispered to Chelle. We were halfway up the mountain.

"Are you sure?" she asked. When I nodded, she stopped and set me down.

"Thank you. I don't know—I don't know what that was." I looked down at my hands. "I have never felt anything like that before. I just got so angry, and I can't—Chelle, I can't lose anyone else. I can't lose you."

She wrapped me in a hug. "You're not going to lose me. Remember, even if we die, we'll meet again in Persephone's palace."

I shook my head. "But you're not going to die, right? You're not—"

"I'm not going to die, Rose. We're going to be together for a very long time."

It was a lie, a beautiful lie. She couldn't predict whether she was going to die or not, any more than anyone else could, but I needed to hear it. I needed to hear that she wanted to live, and that she had every intention of living, no matter what the universe had in store for us.

"Rama, before he—he told me about a place we can go to be safe. It's the world where he was born."

Chelle scratched her head. "I thought he was born on Earth. That's what the stories say."

"Oh, that's nonsense." We started to walk up the mountain again. "The gods, their stories traveled all over the universe, morphing and changing with every world they built, and every culture they helped develop. Rama was no more a product of Earth than any of the other gods of legend."

"That explains a lot."

The path was steep and tiring, but not impossible to navigate. The closer we got to the Spindle, the steeper the path became, and I began to breathe heavily. Finally, I sat on a rock that jutted out of the ground.

"I need to stop for a minute."

Chelle looked up at the mountain. "Can't you just fly us out there?"

"Probably, actually," I replied. "But I'm not myself. I depleted my magic. I feel really weighed down."

"Maybe I can do it, then. I can't fly, but I can do something."

Chelle slammed her hand into the ground and a large rock crashed into the path. She gestured for me to sit on it, and when I did, she pushed the ground, and the rock began to move us toward the top of the hill. After a few minutes, we reached the plateau where the Obsidian Spindle stood.

I chuckled, brushing myself off. "That was nice. We should have done it sooner."

"Well, I was saving my magic for a big fight, but it seems like you scared them off."

"That doesn't sound like—" My eyes narrowed. It wasn't like the Spore to be scared off about anything.

"Well, you sure took a long time," a shrill voice cracked through the air. When we regained our balance, we were face to face with Nox. "I got your message, and I have to say I'm disappointed that you think me so cowardly that killing a few of us would stop a mission I have been trying to accomplish for a billion years."

"You've failed for a billion years?" Chelle snorted. "You must be very bad at your job."

"Failure is a part of life. If you deny it, you can never find success."

"That sounds like failure talk," Chelle said.

Nox shrugged. "I am just very patient. I knew eventually the gods would slip up and give me enough power to fulfill my plan. After all, I can fail a million times, but I only have to succeed once."

"Well, it won't be this time," I growled.

She cackled. "My poor, dear, misguided child. I feel the magical energy dripping off you, and it's barely a whisper of what it was just a few hours ago. You need time to refill your well. That's the difference between you and me. I have the entirety of the cosmos at my disposal."

"And so do I!" Kadlu shouted as she leapt over the hill, covered in muck and grime. She turned to us with a smile. "I'm sorry I took so long. I was tied up."

"Bravo!" Nox said, clapping. "Now, this is almost a fair fight."

"Enough talk," I said. "Move aside and we won't kill you."

Chelle gripped her dagger tight. "I'm definitely not making that promise."

Kadlu spun her bow. "Me either."

"Then let's begin," Nox said with a coy smile on her face.

CHAPTER 20
NIMUE

The other princesses dashed across the city looking for Red, but I had a different matter to resolve. Baba spoke to the being controlling Nox as if they were old, ancient acquaintances. The hag was old even when this place was young, and the records she had were an incredibly powerful resource, if they could be found. Maybe, there would even be a way to destroy whatever had taken control of Nox.

I made a summoning circle in the ground around Baba's body and muttered a spell to speak with the dead. I had heard it a hundred times in my youth, in the hills of Romania.

"*Chem pe mortii care numesc acest loc acasa,*" I said, over and over again, until the ground rumbled and a spirit broke through the ground, screaming bloody murder.

"You!" Baba pointed at me. "You dare call for me?"

"I do," I replied. "We do not like each other, but I doubt you like the Spore much more."

"I kept their secrets, even when—but now, no, I do not care for them, after my allegiance has brought me nothing but death."

"Then help me defeat them, as payment for Nox killing you."

"That was not Nox. It was the Spore."

"Who are the Spore?"

"Why should I help you? You already betrayed me once."

"Because no one else will allow you to get justice for your death. I am offering you something none other will ever bring to you, and if you do not accept my help, you will never find peace."

"Perhaps you are right, traitor." She nodded. "Very well. The Spore is the last Primordial left on this plane. My sister and I cared for it, and it granted us abnormally long life and powers beyond what we could control. It was our loyalty to it that brought us here."

"Do you know how to destroy it?" I asked.

"I do," she said. "We were caretakers for the Spore when the gods destroyed their hosts all over the universe, and in it they told us many things."

"Do you have them written down somewhere?"

She nodded again. "In my library, deep below my house, there is a book that will show you where to find the plant that destroyed the Spore down to all but the last remnant. We kept it to ourselves just in case we needed to come out against the Spore in the end. It looks like our fears were founded."

"Tell me how to get it, and I will deliver it to you."

"I keep a special tea in a tin over my stove. Drink it and it will give you access to the dungeon, where you will find my library, if you are lucky."

"Can you draw me a map?" I asked.

"I could, but I won't, traitor. This is your punishment for betraying me. If you die, you will live in my dungeon forever, tortured by the beasts that have surely made their way out of their cells by now without my magic to contain them. If you survive, then you stand a chance against the Spore."

"That is not much of a help," I replied. "But I suppose it is enough. If Bethel figured it out, so can I."

"Your confidence is delicious. I hope you fail." She grinned. "If you do find a way to succeed and betray the Spore, please let them know it was because of me. They were supposed to save us from the gods, and instead they condemned us to this place, and forced us to work with the gods to save ourselves."

"I will make sure they know before the end."

I stood up and teleported to Baba's house. I followed a path through her yard and pushed open the door to her house, careful to avoid the traps she had laid. If I got caught in her prison, that would be it for me for the rest of my life. Nobody would know where I was, or how to get to me with Baba now dead.

I found the tea above her stove and boiled water. I made sure to drink every drop, and when it was done a glowing white door grew against the far wall. This could have been a trap, very easily, but I couldn't let that possibility invade my thoughts. It was my only option, and if it was a trap, I only hoped it killed me quickly.

CHAPTER 21

ROSE

Kadlu attacked first, swinging her bow in precise strikes that Nox easily dodged. After the first three of them, an explosion of force blew from the tip of the bow and caught Nox unprepared. She was sent flying backward across the ground.

"Pathetic," Nox replied, righting herself.

She raised her hands and made a slashing motion, and two swords made of pure energy cut through the air. Kadlu smashed them both as she leapt forward again with a flip, and barely missed hitting Nox across the nose.

"She's going to get eaten alive out there on her own," Chelle said. She clapped her hands together to create a wall of thunder that knocked into Nox and bowled her over. She quickly recovered, and the shockwave rebounded toward us with double the force.

Chelle knocked me out of the way and took the full brunt of the attack, which sent her to her knees.

"No!" I screamed.

I was tired and my well of magic empty, but I couldn't

let Chelle get hurt. I stood at full attention as stiff as I could and held out my hands. *"Examen apium!"*

The bees swarmed Nox. It wasn't a powerful spell, but I hoped it would be enough to distract her and give Chelle and Kadlu a chance to attack.

"Truly pathetic," Nox replied, flicking the bees out of the air, but not before Kadlu smashed her bow into Nox's stomach. She let out an ungodly scream and toppled over to the ground. She was a powerful mage, but in hand-to-hand combat, perhaps we could defeat her.

"Chelle, the dagger," I said. "Give it to me."

"No way," she growled and held it closer. She hopped up, and when she slashed Nox across the face with it, the black ichor blood burst through the air as a soundwave, sending Kadlu and Chelle flying.

"I have tried to indulge you, because I very much need you alive, but if you insist on being a pest, then I don't need you conscious."

Two spectral hands shot from Nox's body and beat Chelle as she lay on the ground. I picked up the golden dagger from where it had landed at my feet. I used it to slice through the arms, cutting them off at the end. They receded with a guttural scream from Nox.

"You're not taking her!" I shouted.

She cocked her head. "You love her, that much has always been clear, but love is not enough to save somebody from their destiny."

I sneered. "She died once, and it was my love that sent me into the Underworld to look for her. It was my love that made the goddess Nox realize that she needed to bring Chelle back to me. It was our love that has kept us together, so no, you're wrong."

Nox cackled. "Do you really believe that the goddess

cared about you? Chelle coming back to the land of the living was not some great gesture. It was just another part of Nox's plan."

"I don't believe you. There's no way she wanted to work with you."

"She didn't," Nox replied. "Her goal was to tap into the source of our power, and give the gift of creation to all humanity, so that they would be equal to the gods, like Rapunzel, and be able to fight back against the oppression they have been suffering since the dawn of time."

I had to admit, that sounded a lot like Nox.

"It was a foolish plan," she continued. "Could you imagine more of you foolish parasites with the powers of the gods? You would not fight back against your oppressors, you would fight each other, like the vermin you are. If we had known what this universe would become, we never would have created it."

"I'm not going to let you erase us."

Nox raised her hand in the air. "As if you have a choice."

Before she dropped her hand, Kadlu slammed her in the back and leapt on top of her. "Go! Get out of here! I'll keep her distracted."

She would surely die, but I didn't fight her, as much as I should have. Instead, I grabbed Chelle's beaten body and wrapped it over my shoulders.

"*Sana,*" I whispered, trying to heal her as much as possible. The light from the Obsidian Spindle glowed welcomingly as we hobbled away from the sound of the battle. Once we were inside the Spindle, we would figure out how to save the universe, but we couldn't do anything while we were being chased by a lunatic god like whatever Nox had become.

"Enough!" Nox shouted and before I could react, Kadlu

shot into my back and sent me and Chelle both tumbling over. "This has been fun, but I can't let you get away with my prize. You on the other hand, I have no use for."

She raised her hand and fired a bolt of electricity at me. I cringed and held out my hand to release a shield I wasn't sure I could summon, but at the last moment Chelle stepped in front of the bolt and pushed me away.

"Save me," Chelle said, with a smile, even as the lightning coursed through her.

I didn't know what she meant until I spun around and saw myself headed straight for the Obsidian Spindle. I tried to hold myself back, but I tripped over my feet and fell inside. Then it was over, and I felt myself traveling a million miles an hour into the great unknown.

CHAPTER 22
NIMUE

Well, she was right. Her dungeon was certainly dying. It was a part of Baba, and with her death, so went the sinew and cartilage that held together the many cells that wove through the rooms..

The low growl of monsters filled the halls, and more laid dead on the ground. They were fighting for dominance. Baba probably kept them hungry to the point of starvation. They would be after me soon enough.

"Wha—what are you doing here?" a voice called. I turned to see a ghost. It was Elvira, complete with her pale white skin and six horns. Her eyes were a pale shade of red, and I could see through her to the other side of the prison, but it was assuredly her.

"Elvira." I cupped my hand to my mouth. "What have they done to you?"

"The dogs found me, and I thought I would die, but then I saw Baba. She took one look at me, smiled, and then pushed me out of my own body so that she could take over. Since then, I have wandered the halls until earlier today, when the whole place started falling apart, and it was every beast for itself."

"Baba is dead, and with it, so is your body."

Elvira looked down at her hands. "I was wondering why I had faded so much. I hope I am not long for this plane of existence."

"Perhaps you can help me before you go. I am looking for a library that can show me how to kill a great evil that has lived for billions of years, infecting millions."

Elvira sighed. "You speak of the Spore."

"Yes...that's right. How did you know that?"

"I don't know, but an image of them flashed through my mind just now. Perhaps it's because Baba took over my body, or something about the magic of this place, but I know many things I should not. For instance, I knew you defeated Hastur, though I have never left this place to see it." She clasped her hands together. "Tell me, did he weep at the end? Did he beg for his life? Did he whimper for salvation?"

"No," I replied. "He died a clean death, but he took Bethel down with him. It would have been honorable if he had any honor." I swallowed my grief. "You did a great job, and I am so grateful for it. His death opened a door back to the universe, and we can rejoin our brethren, now, all thanks to you and her sacrifice."

Elvira simply looked down at her hands and smiled. "I have so rarely done anything good in my life, it is nice to know that my death meant something."

"It can mean more," I replied. "If you can show me to the library where I might find more information on the Spore."

Elvira's eyes rolled to the back of her head for a moment, and then she nodded. "I believe I can show you the way. Watch yourself, the monsters of this place should not attack while I am with you. They sense I am one of them, damned and forgotten, but do not leave the path I chart for you."

I followed her through the sinew of the cells, the smell of rotten, death flesh filling my nostrils. Huge monsters, warped bears, rabid wolves, and all manner of beast too horrible to recount filled the hallways, chomping on their fallen comrades, resting in packs, and eyeing me as I passed.

"These are circuitous tunnels without a map, and whoever told you to come here surely meant for you to find your death."

"It was Baba's ghost."

"Yes, then the venom she feels for you makes sense. She must not have known you would find me here, or she never would have sent you here."

We turned through labyrinthian hallways until finally, we reached a spiral staircase that led into deep shadow. Elvira lit a purple, glowing fire in her hand and headed down. The wind whipped and our steps echoed through the stone. At the bottom was a library much smaller than I expected to find. Elvira reached forward and ran her fingers over the leather-bound volumes, before stopping on one bound in red leather.

"This one."

I grabbed the book, my hand floating right through Elvira's. There couldn't have been more than fifty pages, and it was tiny. Inside, the pages were covered with a messy scrawl in foreign words. I squinted. "I can't read this."

"Here," she said. "Maybe this will help."

Elvira touched the book and leeched herself into it. When she was done, her soul was nowhere to be found, but the book glowed, and the letters reformed into a language I could understand.

"Thank you," I said.

"Keep me close and I will help you as I'm able, in the final fight that is to come with the Spore. Meanwhile, I will mark the page you need to form the glyph that will kill the Spore for good."

"Thank you, sister."

ARIEL

"Have you killed anyone since coming to the Dream Realm?" I asked Canterbury. His Seeker carried us, easily climbing the gem-walls of the city.

"Of course not!" Canterbury scoffed. "I just wanted to find my friend and see if he was happy. Won't lie, though. Knowing he is dead creates a powerful anger in me, though."

"In me too, rabbit."

From the top of the wall, I could see all the Emerald City in ruins. Fires burned uncontrollably, and the shrieks of citizens filled the air. I only hoped that the sword that Hypnos told me to find would give the Dream Realm the glimmer of hope they needed.

"Damn shame, isn't it?" Canterbury said. "We're not so different, our realms, but when we come together, it's like oil and water."

"We are nothing alike. The Dream Realm is a peaceful place."

"For you, but I'll bet there's plenty of strife if you look

past your own experience. Monsters and humans could live together, though. I know because I lived with Kelvin peacefully, and there were whole colonies in Sprig where monsters co-existed with humans." He turned toward the ocean. "Let's go, buddy."

The Seeker headed down the embankment toward the sea. When I could feel the salt air on my skin, he scooped me from his shoulder and dropped me to the ground.

"Thank you," I said. "What will you do now?"

"I don't know," he replied. "I think Kelvin would want me to save some people, if I could."

"You held him in high opinion, even though he ruled the Nightmare Realm with an iron fist."

"It is the kind of place you can't rule gently, Ariel," Canterbury said. "You either rule with a tight fist or not at all, but here—I really think he would have liked it here."

"I hope when this is over you can make a life here, to honor him."

"I think he would have liked that. There's nothing left for me in the Nightmare Realm. Not anymore."

I said my final goodbyes and dove into the Forgotten Sea. I cast extra speed on myself as I swam down into the depths, and soon enough the light from the sky dissipated. It wasn't long before I found the head of my adopted mother's army, but this time they did not let me through peacefully. Instead, they swarmed in any direction I tried to travel, blocking me from the depths, until a familiar mermaid with great, bulging blue eyes stopped me.

"Your mother requests an audience," he said.

"And I suppose this is not a request, so much as an order. Right, Caligan?" I replied, as full of power as I could muster.

"You remember the ways of the sea well, even after all this time."

"I do not belong here," I replied.

"In that we agree."

When Caligan turned, the mermaids parted, and as we moved through, several squads peeled off to join us. They must have heard about my fight with Vivian, and how powerful I had become since receiving Hypnos's blessing.

In less than an hour, we were outside Ursula's throne room. It had once been such an inviting place, but now it filled me with dread.

"Do not make eye contact with the queen," Caligan said, his words dripping with contempt. "And only speak when spoken to, human."

"I know how to speak to my mother," I growled.

The door opened and bubbles filled the room. When they dissipated, we entered. The look on my mother's face was horrible and stern. It had none of the love she once had for me, but then, maybe that was just a dream.

"Where is my daughter, Ariel?" the queen asked, holding the scepter that Vivian had taken from Nox's vault. "Did Hypnos really think this trinket would be enough to appease me?"

"I don't think he cared much what you thought, Ursula." There was no reason to lie. "Your daughter plotted with Loki to destroy Hypnos and take Urgu for themselves. You can't possibly expect the lord of dreams to let her go after that."

"I expect him to respect my power as he does the queen of fairies that sits on her ill-gotten throne."

"I can't believe you're worried about Vivian when the whole of the Dream Realm is under attack by monsters from the Nightmare Realm. There are bigger things to worry about than your pride."

"How dare you, girl!" She slammed the scepter on the ground. "I did everything for you, and this is how you treat me?"

"You did nothing except hide me away like a prisoner!" I cried.

"For your safety!"

"Yes, you would believe that." I bit my lip. "I really am very busy, so is there anything else?"

"I will have satisfaction," she shouted.

"No," I replied. "You will never be satisfied. I know that now." I floated off the ground. "No matter, if there is nothing else then—"

"I want my daughter back!"

I turned to leave. "I don't have time for this pettiness."

Ursula laughed. "You think you will leave when my favorite daughter is in shackles! Guards!"

"Do not test me!" I created a fireball in my hand and looked up at her. The water boiled around it, but it wasn't extinguished. "I will walk out that door, free and clear, to handle my business, or you will make a powerful enemy this day."

"You dare threaten me?"

I couldn't believe it, either. "I have too much riding on my shoulders to get caught up in your vanity. The fate of Urgu —no, of the whole universe, hangs in the balance, and I do not have the energy to add your petulance to my list of cares."

I headed out the door, half expecting the guards to cause a scene but instead they simply looked at their queen.

"If you leave this place, never come back again, or you

will be treated like a common enemy," Ursula said, narrowing her eyes, "and you know what we do with our enemies."

"I never intend to come back, Mother, and when I walk through that door, please forget I ever existed."

CHAPTER 24

RED

"Hop in," Virtrund said as he pulled himself into the cab of his wagon. "It's not much, but it's gotten better than you out of Carcosa before."

I didn't acknowledge his jab, but he didn't seem to care either way. "I know this is an inconvenience, and I appreciate you helping me."

"Inconvenience doesn't do justice to what you're asking, stranger," Virtrund said. "If I didn't think Yriz would keep trying to help you until she got herself killed, I'd turn you away, but she was always a better woman than even my brother deserved. I'm doing this for her, not for you."

"I don't rightly care why you are doing it, as long as it's getting done."

"No, I don't suppose you would."

He cracked the whip and the enormous wolves with pig snouts started to move forward. I hadn't been in a drawn wagon in a long time, and it was rightly boring in a way I couldn't quite describe. After snapping around the universe, using cars, planes, and fairy doors, among other things, seeing the world at two horsepower—or wolf power—was a bit tedious.

"Don't suppose you have any money," Virtrund asked as we turned down a cobblestone street.

I reached into my coin purse and pulled out several shining silver pieces, and a few gold. Random assortments of gods and kings had been molded into them, and no two looked exactly the same. They were my only souvenir of my journey through the cosmos. I had seen and done so much and yet, it felt like I was still that little girl fighting for Ozma all those years ago. I placed them on the bench between us for him to examine.

"Maybe I can bring them to a smelter, and they can make something useful with all that," Virtrund said as he pawed through my coins. "Won't do us much good now."

"I'm sorry. I don't want to be a bother."

His thousand eyes narrowed. "No? You look like the type that always causes a bother whether she wants to or not."

"You might be right there," I replied, scratching my head. "Still, I would much rather not have involved you in this."

Virtrund sighed. "Well, I am involved, and since I'm involved, this is how it's going to work. In about two minutes we're going to turn the corner and stop at a gate." He reached under his seat and pulled out two manacles. "They're going to ask me where I'm going, and no matter what I say, just reply, don't speak unless I explicitly ask you a question. Even then, say 'yes, sir.' Humans like you are meant to be seen and not heard, but you have a pair of lips on you that are bound to disobey. Got it?"

"I can do what I'm told, sir." I looked him in the face. "I won't cause any trouble for you."

"You've already caused a heap of trouble, but I'd appreciate you not causing anymore. Now, let's try it. When I talk, what do you say?"

"Nothing."

"Good," he replied. "Though I would have preferred you stay silent. Now, when I ask you a question, what do you say?"

"Yes, sir."

"Perfect." He pulled the hood over my head. "And keep your head down for crying out loud, and act deferential for a change, will you?"

"Yes, sir," I growled. "And what if somebody else talks to me?"

"Let's just keep it easy and say 'yes, sir' to anyone we come across."

"What if there's a woman?"

"How will you be able to tell, human?" he growled. "Enough. Now look sad already."

I snapped on the manacles and made sure they were prominently visible. Then I slumped my shoulders and pulled the hood over my face. As we turned the corner, Virtrund locked the manacles into place at the base of his wagon.

"Soloman!" He waved at the orc with an elephant's nose that guarded the gate.

"Virtrund, my friend." The orc smiled. "Leaving the city again so soon?"

This was where the rubber met the road, as they said, even though the wagon wheels were made of wood and metal. Virtrund could have easily turned me in to the guards and gotten a hefty reward for his trouble, I would wager. I had put my faith in Yriz, and that she was a good judge of character, so I only hoped my instinct was correct, especially since the manacles were locked to the base of the wagon and I had no way of picking their lock.

Virtrund let out a fake, annoyed sigh. "I have business down south, bringing this one to the market, along with some other pieces to trade."

Soloman turned his attention to me. "Doesn't look like much."

"That's because she isn't, but there's slim pickings down in Emder, so they'll take what they can get, I hope. Otherwise, it will be a waste of time."

Soloman pulled out a clipboard. "Alright, Virtrund. Well, I'm just going to have to ask you a couple of questions."

Virtrund reached into his pocket and pulled out some coin. He reached down and handed it to Soloman. "Is that really necessary, between old friends?"

Soloman smiled. "You must really need to keep this under the radar if you're willing to give me ten quat off the top. Usually you negotiate a bit."

"I'm in no mood today." Virtrund shrugged. "I need to keep this business secret, okay?"

Soloman eyed me up and down. "You have a good master here for the time being, you know that?"

I turned to Virtrund, who nodded, giving me permission to speak. He didn't say it was necessary to do that, but I thought it was a nice touch. "Yes, sir."

Soloman turned back to Virtrund. "I guess we can let this slide, for old time's sake."

"Wonderful!" Virtrund said. "Stop by my shop in two weeks' time and I will bring back some mead for you and your wife, and a toy for your little one."

"I will," Soloman replied. "And be careful out there. The wilds are no place for humans."

"Brother," Virtrund replied. "You just said a mouthful."

I rolled Kadlu off me and looked up in horror at the monster staring down at me. *Nox.*

Her eyes were more sunken than I remembered from our last meeting, and she had a crazed, wild frenzy about her. Maniacal, almost.

"Don't be scared, child. Death is not so bad. I have died millions of times on thousands of different worlds."

"I've died, too, and let me tell you, if you aren't afraid of death, you're a moron."

She chuckled. "You have as much verve as the other one. I hate it."

I crawled back toward the Obsidian Spindle. Along the way my finger brushed against Kadlu's bow. "I don't care."

I pulled the bow from my side and swung it across Nox's face, then rushed to the Spindle. I leapt toward it, but the light had dissipated, leaving nothing but black rock in its place.

"I think not," Nox said, wiping some black ichor from her mouth. "Good try, though."

She twisted her outstretched hand and I rose into the

air, my arms locked into place. I squirmed to break free, but I already knew it wasn't possible unless I could break her concentration.

"Get off her!"

Kadlu punched Nox in the rib and then across the face, and I dropped to the ground. The Obsidian Spindle wasn't glowing, so I leapt down the hill looking for anywhere safe.

That's when I saw the twenty gods floating in the air, their eyes a haunting black, waiting to pounce. Even if we could defeat Nox, there would be no fighting the gods.

"Do you see how futile it is?" Nox asked. Kadlu was limp in her hands. With the flick of her wrist, Nox threw her off the edge of the cliff to the unwelcoming ground hundreds of feet below.

"I would rather die than—"

Nox cracked me across the face before I could finish. I fell backwards and found myself cradled by two glowing arms.

"You will get your chance to die," Nox said. "Don't worry about that."

And with that, the lights went out, and I slipped into darkness. My last thoughts were of Rose, and how she would have to save me yet again. If she didn't, the whole universe would be destroyed.

I love you, Rose.

CHAPTER 26
NIMUE

I felt quite satisfied with myself as I exited the prison, not only because I had found a way to defeat the newest enemy threatening my power, but also because the prison was the last vestige of Baba on The Dark Planet, and now I knew she was truly gone. Yet another enemy had fallen at my feet while I still drew breath. The Spore didn't know who they were dealing with.

This was not the first time a powerful being had tried to force their will upon me, and at every turn they had fallen, while I lived. Hera, Epiales, Rapunzel, Hastur, Baba, and now, the Spore. If they thought me some simple queen with simple powers and woeful aims, they were mistaken. I had survived the will of the gods before, and I would survive that will of the Primordials as well. If they found a way through the barrier and into our universe, I would worm my way into some form of power in the new normal, just as I had in the Dream Realm, the Nightmare Realm, the Fairy Realm, and the Dark Planet. Even when my plans did not survive, I did. The Spore were powerful, of that I was sure, but so were all who crossed me.

I exited Baba's shack and teleported back to the remains of the castle.

"Nimue!" The pain of Lydia's voice echoed in my head like a hellish migraine, but I turned to her with a smile.

"Good to see you, Lydia. Did you find our runaway?"

"Not quite, but you should come with me now."

I followed her across the rooftops of Carcosa. It might not save us much time taking the rooftops, but it meant we didn't have to deal with the peasant class, and it looked impressive. Perception was very important when creating a mythos around yourself, maybe the most important thing. If people saw you walking amongst them, it might create the impression that you were approachable and tell your enemies that you were vulnerable.

The denizens of the city stifled screams and looked at us with the kind of fear I'd forgotten I missed. It was one thing to be loved, but people turned on those they loved. If they feared you, it was much easier to gain their servitude. They would think hard before turning against you.

Word had spread through the city of Hastur's death by now, to be sure. They pointed and whispered to each other as we continued. Most of them cowered from us, but a few smiled at the sight of their liberators. They had no idea whether we would be righteous rulers, or if the king's death would create a power vacuum that could only be filled with a bloody war, or another reign of terror.

"Where are you taking me?" I asked as we traveled across half the city.

"We found a traitor in our search of the city who took coin to let criminals through the gates of the city. Delilah is working to break him now, and we know how effective she is at that type of thing."

When we reached the far end of the city we jumped down to the cobbles.

Lydia pushed open the door to a guard tower. In a chair at the center of the room was a great orc with the trunk of an elephant. He screamed out in pain as Delilah shocked him through his nipples with a bolt of lightning. He lit up blue and shook violently.

"Is he ready?" Lydia asked, now her words echoing through both our brains.

"If he's not, he'll be dead soon," Delilah growled.

"I'll talk," the elephant-trunked man blubbered. "I'll tell you anything."

Lydia put her face next to his. "Do you know who I am?"

He nodded. "Of course, you are the princesses, all of you."

"Correct, so you know what will happen if you lie to me." She brought her hand to the galaxy swirling around her head. "I'll know."

They didn't need to torture the poor soldier, since Lydia simply could have known if he was lying, but it was what Delilah loved most in the world.

"I won't lie. I swear."

Lydia paced in front of him. "Earlier today you let a Herphaloid pass without inspection, yes?"

He sniffled miserably. "Virtrund is a friend of mine. He told me he was talking to a girl to be sold in the south. It seemed legit to me."

Lydia reached into her cape and pulled out a rendering of Gabrielle. "Was this the woman?"

The elephant man looked at the picture. "It—could have been. I don't—she was under a cloak."

"I tire of this." Lydia let the paper drop to the floor and touched the sides of the man's head. The man jostled violently, then fell silent as his body grew rigid. Lydia held him that way for more than a minute, and then her hands dropped. When they did, the man's head fell limp as well.

"It was her," Lydia said. "She has a couple hours' head-start. We should be able to catch up with her without issue. Neither of them has any powers to speak of, and they traveled alone on a single cart pulled by dire wolves."

"Wonderful," Elvira said. "I grow tired of this place anyway."

"Then dispose of this body and let us away," Lydia said.

"So, he's dead?" I asked, little emotion in my voice.

"Yes," Lydia said. "It is the curse and the blessing of my power. I can enter any brain, but when I am done, it severs the mind from the body. Good riddance. His life was terrible anyway, and he was cheating on his wife. We will give a pittance to the family, and then move on."

"I'm not cleaning him up," Delilah said. "I kept him alive. Your mess, your responsibility."

Lydia growled. "We will get the guards to do it. It will be a good show of our force to keep the military in line."

CHAPTER 27

ROSE

The portal spat me out on the floor of the terminal at the center of the Celestial Realm. The whole station had been abandoned, and a cold chill emphasized the haunting silence.

Kadlu. Chelle. I had left them to the whims of Nox's invasion force. I needed to get back to the planet immediately.

I leapt up and examined the portal, looking for a way back to them, but it was closed, nothing but black rock, an oddity in the collection of white doors that led across the universe. I didn't know the name of the planet, or how to get there even if I did.

There had to be another way back. Maybe if I returned to Rama's house, I could find out how to operate the controls in his massive library. Then at least I would be hidden from the Spore. I found my feet and rushed to the edge of the terminal, just as two gods came out from the white portals into the main chamber of the terminal.

"I don't see her," one of them said, gruffly.

"She came this way," the other replied. "We saw it through the main's eyes."

"Perhaps she made her way out of the city into another planet," the first said. She had a thick, tangled mane of hair, and a pinched face.

The other was a man, shorter but dense, holding a battle axe with glowing blue runes on it. "Possible. Let's try the other portals, and we'll send others to search the city for her."

They disappeared into two different portals and were gone. My sigh of relief was short-lived, as four more gods dropped down at the entrance. I didn't wait for them to talk before I slid into the shadows.

"*Umbra*," I muttered, touching my chest. The shadows shrouded me. In the Celestial Realm, I felt my powers grow, but they were still not full. My soul felt like it had been split in two.

The path across the city was treacherous, with black-eyed Spore gods roaming every street. There was no casual strolling between them. They all walked with purpose, their heads swiveling as they moved, tracking every movement.

The gods had ways of seeing through my magic, so I took off my shoes and pulled my clothing tight so that it wouldn't make the slightest rustle. The good news was that they weren't looking for me specifically. They seemed to be searching for anyone that wasn't already in their thrall.

"Stop!" a voice whinnied as two gods pulled a centaur from a house and threw him at the feet of a stone-faced goddess in the center of the square. I recognized the centaur as the lawyer who had been kind to me once, when I was new to the Celestial Realm.

The goddess opened her mouth wide, and a black mass

of Spore, like the ones I'd seen fly out of Rama's mouth, shot from her throat and into the centaur's. He jerked violently for a second, and then was still.

"There," he said in a calm voice. "That's better." He righted himself and looked around. "You three, go look for others. I'll continue down this road a bit, and then meet you at the Oracle."

The Oracle? That was something I hadn't heard of, but it sounded important. Maybe a home base for the Spore? Whatever it was, I needed to stay away from it until I had more information. I waited until the group disbanded and then crept across the street into the building they had just vacated. It wasn't a perfect cover, but they had already checked it recently, so it was as good a place to catch my breath as any. The cloaking spell drained my energy and made me feel like I had the flu.

The offices inside the two-story building were plain, with nothing of note in the way of décor, which was notable in and of itself, as the gods had a flair for the dramatic. I reached the top of the stairs and perched near a window, looking down at the street. It was as empty as the terminal.

They seemed to be rounding up anyone who wasn't one of them, but for what specific purpose? If I had to guess, it would be to guard whatever weapon they were going to use to carry out their dastardly plan.

In the silence I heard something, but it didn't activate my fear senses. It sounded like crying. I searched for it until I found its source in a small closet in the bathroom. A small centaur, a little girl, huddled there whimpering.

"Hey, it's okay." I held up my hands. "I'm not here to hurt you."

She looked at me with bloodshot eyes. "You're not?"

"No, I'm not. Was that your father that they took?"

She bit her lip and squeezed her eyes shut, the tears falling harder. "Yes."

"Hey, hey, it's going to be okay."

She shook her head. "Daddy said it would all be okay, too, but nothing is okay. He's gone now, isn't he?"

"He is, and I'll bet you're scared, huh?" I sat down on the floor of the cold bathroom. "I've helped a lot of worlds that didn't seem like they would ever be okay, and they are now. I'm going to help you, too."

"What can you do?" She sneered. "You're just a human."

I laughed. "Yeah, well you would be surprised what humans can do."

"No, I wouldn't. Daddy says you destroy everything you touch."

"He's not wrong," I replied. "But we save some things, too, on our good days. I promise I'm not going to rest until I save your daddy, okay?"

She wiped her eyes. "Really?"

"Really." I smiled at her. "Now, I'm going to my friend's house. It's safe there. Do you want to come with me?"

"Yes."

I held out my hand. "Then, I'm Rose. I hope we can be friends."

"I'm Blanche." She took my hand and shook it.

"I need you to be brave, Blanche. Can you do that?"

"I—I don't know."

"I know exactly how you feel. I'm scared every minute of every day, but I know something about bravery, too. Bravery is all about being scared but doing it anyway. Can you do that, Blanche?"

She wiped her nose with her forearm. "I—I think so."

"That's a good girl."

CHAPTER 28
ARIEL

I didn't have much time left. I felt that deep in my soul. I needed to find the Hope Bringer sword quickly if I was to have a chance of saving Urgu.

I had swam the path to Nox's cavern many hundreds of times over my long life in Ursula's kingdom, and I made it there with little effort. The mermaids I passed looked at me with distrust and ire, but they did not attack. I was never one of them, but Ursula's protection forced them to treat me with a kindness I now knew was false. I was never one of them, just an entitled prisoner who wasted her life oblivious to the truth of her existence.

Rocks still guarded the entrance to the cave from when I brought them down upon Vivian. With Hypnos's blessing, it was nothing to move them away and swim through. The path grew narrower, and I turned right and left through the watery maze as I remembered Vivian had done, though I feared I would be stuck in the arteries of the tight corridors forever if I made a single wrong move. The current pushed me faster through the rocky corridors until a small vein opened above me and I followed it into a small pool.

I exited the water and walked toward the room that Nox kept for her secret tryst with Vivian. Had either of them cared about each other, in truth, or was it a relationship built of convenience? Was Vivian capable of love for any but herself, or was she simply attracted to power like a moth to a flickering flame?

I passed the bed they'd shared, and the desk where we found the secret to opening the vault. The last time it took two of us to open the door, but the rage I felt inside my belly for my capture, for my betrayals, for the trust I put in other people, burned brightly, and with the power Hypnos granted me, the vault snapped open for me without any other help.

The wreckage of my fight with Vivian remained all around the floor of the vault. Dotting the path to the sword were heaps of armor and weapons that I had flung toward her, toppled shelving, and the remnants of the shadows that she called forth.

I found the ledger Nox made to inventory all her treasure and turned the pages until I found an entry for "Hope Bringer sword – TNJCY-1297." I followed the shelves, weaving between them to find the place Nox had indicated.

Only one problem—when I reached the shelf, it was gone.

CHAPTER 29

RED

If I get out of this alive, I swear to the gods that I will never, ever ask for a life filled with action again. I know I have said that before, but honestly and truly, I will be so happy with a very, small, boring life. I will complain about it, but I will not go searching it out. I will not let my bitterness get the best of me. I won't, I won't, I won't.

Who was I trying to kid? This was my life. I was never happy without an adventure. Even when the whole of the world was against me—even when the whole universe was against me, it was better than a normal, boring life.

But at least a boring life was a life...continuing to get caught up in this ridiculousness...it would lead to my death, for certain this time. I died once before, and I woke up in the Dream Realm. Maybe the Underworld wasn't so bad, but I had a feeling I wasn't going there this time. Where did pure magical energy go when it died? Did it flake away into the universe? Did it matter? At least then there would be no more worlds to save, and I could find peace.

"You have been quiet for a long time, little one," Virtrund said over the sound of the dire wolves.

"I'm sorry. I'm just thinking."

He grunted. The animals pulling the carriage groaned. "The road is a good place for that. Somewhere between the methodic trotting of the horses, and the rhythmic clang of the reins, and the wind whipping against your face—there is a peace in it that brings forth thought. Good ones, I hope."

The cart jerked forward, and I pursed my lips. "Not especially good or bad. Just thinking about death, like always, and trying to figure out how I keep getting myself in these crazy situations."

"You seem to have a good heart. I would imagine that's where the problem lies."

"Most people wouldn't think that's a problem." I turned toward the scenery out the window. The mangled trees of the Dark Planet passed slowly in the distance, as twisted and gnarled as Nimue's cold heart. "I've seen much more problems from people with bad hearts, like Nimue."

"Yes, but the problem with a good heart is that when it sees evil, it can't turn away from it, which gets you into trouble. The same failing was true in my brother as well."

"Seems like the kind of person I would like to know."

He shrugged. The dire wolves snarled as the cart listed from side to side. "Maybe, but his good heart nearly got his wife and child killed, and Ariz's good heart could lead to her daughter's death, which is the last piece of him left in this world. Imagine if the whole of you was taken out of this world."

"I don't have to imagine much. My family died a long time ago, and I am the last I know of my kin."

"And yet you still take such risks?" He shook his head. "I know it is not a proud life for most, but I appreciate those who can plant roots and tend them in one place, never causing trouble, and always looking out to foster the next in their line. I wish I was such a person."

"So, your good heart gets you in just as much trouble as mine gets me?"

He thought for a long moment. "I used to be idealistic like my brother. My mother and father told me that I should focus on my chores and keep my head down. They repeated those words all the way to the gallows. The day my father took the blame for my brother's reckless anarchy against the crown, my heart broken open, and it didn't even have a chance to scab over before my mother joined him in death. That was enough to quench my recklessness for a generation, but my brother—he only became more so."

"And yet you are bringing me out of the city." My eye caught a bird with four wings, dark as the night, cutting across the sky. It was beautiful in its twisted deformity. "Doesn't that run counter to what you just told me?"

"It sure does. Part of that is to honor my brother, but as I told you, the bigger part is because you are trouble, and I want to protect his lineage. I don't have one of my own, and so all I have is his. I won't let you destroy it."

"I wouldn—"

A fireball whistled through the air and crashed in front of us. The dire wolves pulled back and bucked and screamed bloody murder. The cart spun as they did their best to turn away from the fire. In their haste, the tire snapped from the pressure and the cart crashed onto its side, throwing me to the ground. It slid into a ditch, and the dire wolves took off across the plains.

"Red," a familiar voice said. I pushed myself up from the dirt and turned to see Nimue floating in the air flanked by three other monsters. "So nice to see you again."

Maybe Virtrund was right. Maybe I was trouble with a

capital T. No, there wasn't a maybe about it. I was definitely trouble, and I destroyed nearly everything I touched, from Ozma on down the line. And now, trouble was here for me again.

I don't know if you ever got used to being knocked out and waking up in weird locations, but if it was possible for somebody to at least acquiesce to the experience, then I had, even though it still royally pissed me off.

When I came to, I found myself bound by metal clamps to an upright table on the edge of a great circular room not totally dissimilar from a planetarium. Computers beeped and chugged along all along the walls, and wires snaked across the room toward us. I felt them connect to the base of my head, and felt electrodes stuck under my shirt, and on my legs.

"Oh good," a smarmy looking god said, walking toward me in a blue lab coat from across the room. "I was hoping we didn't hurt you too badly."

"Leave her alone, Ukko," Hypnos growled. He was on another table next to me, bound the same way I was.

Ukko cocked his head. "I don't know why you insist on calling us by his name. We are Spore. Are your brains really so small to not be able to hold that inside of your head?"

"Yes, they are," I chuckled. I couldn't help but laugh at

somebody taking a god to task, even if we were enemies. I hated the gods oh so much.

"Hey!" Hypos said. "I'm trying to defend you."

"You're the reason I'm here in the first place!" I snapped back. "Not only that, but your stupid blessing nearly destroyed my poor girlfriend's soul. Besides, he's right. You are thick headed like whoa."

"Still, we're supposed to be on the same side. The enemy of my enemy is my friend, after all."

"No, the enemy of my enemy is still my enemy." I rolled my eyes. "I tolerate you, and that's all."

Ukko chuckled. "That is very funny. I'm almost sorry we have to kill you."

"You don't have to do anything, Spore," I replied. "You're trying to kill me so you can bring back your family. You can literally stop at any time."

He shrugged. "You're not wrong, but when you have worked so hard and so long on something, it's hard to shake it from your brain, even if you wanted to, and we don't want to."

I looked past Hypnos to find a slumped over young girl with frizzled red hair. "Who's that?"

"Another of our sacrifices," Ukko said. "I believe she is called Ariel. She has been like that for a while. All the better, since talking is tiresome."

"Then are we the ones you need to destroy the universe? Are you going to kill us soon?"

Ukko shook his head. "No, we're still waiting on one. I believe you know the one called Gabrielle, though some call her Red. She has proven to be more slippery than we anticipated, but we have people working to find her while we finalize our plans."

I smirked. "You're never going to find her."

"We are many, and we are not as thick headed as your god friends here. I believe she will be with us soon, and if not, well, we are a patient being." Ukko looked back to two others who were futzing with the computers. "If you'll excuse me. I have other things to attend."

Ukko exited the room, leaving me alone with Ariel and Hypnos.

I bit my lip, fuming. "That's really annoying."

"Tell me about it. He does it a lot."

"Really? How about you be useful and tell me how often he leaves the room?"

"He's in and out throughout the day, but we're alone for hours at a time sometimes. That's how I was able to send Ariel into the Dream Realm."

"That's where she is now?" I asked. When he nodded, I narrowed my eyes. "Why?"

"I believe my mother, or the being pretending to be her, has started a cascading effect which will destroy the barrier between the Dream Realm and the universe at large. I have sent Ariel to strengthen the barrier and save my people."

"Oh, great," I replied. "Well, that's one less thing to worry about."

Just as I said that, the metal bands on my hands released. I rubbed my wrists together to get the blood flowing in my hands again.

Hypnos's eyes widened. "How did you—"

Albie hissed at him and I grinned. "They never properly plan for the hair."

"Incredible."

I wedged my hand until the foot clamp and found the failsafe button. I pushed it and my legs fell free. I dropped to the floor and caught myself from falling down.

"I know I am." I walked toward him. "Now, just know

I'm only saving you because that's what Rose would want. I couldn't care less if they kill you or not."

"That's pleasant," Hypnos said.

"You're not infected with the Spore, are you?"

"Not that I know of."

"I guess that's gotta be enough, huh?" I pressed the buttons and Hypnos dropped to the ground. "Any idea why they didn't contaminate you?"

"I don't know. I like to believe that my mother has convinced them to let me alone, but I believe they know I am relatively weak outside of the Dream Realm, so maybe I'm just not a threat."

"Or maybe they know you're a coward who forces young girls to do your dirty work."

Hypnos opened his mouth to protest, but then he dropped his head. "Yes, there is that, too."

"I can't believe you admitted it." I pressed the buttons on Ariel's arms, and she fell into my arms. "Help me carry her. We have to go now."

"It's very dangerous to move a Dreamer."

I pressed the buttons on her legs and caught her weight. "Trust me, it's much more dangerous to leave her here."

"Fair enough."

CHAPTER 31
RED

Virtrund laid on the ground next to his downed cart, breathing heavily and oozing orange bile from the back of his head.

"Virtrund!" I shouted, skidding in the dirt to reach him. I kneeled down. "Are you okay?"

"Absolutely"—he coughed—"not."

"It's a pity what happened to your new friend," Nimue said, landing a few yards from me. "Why do you kill everything that comes near you?"

It was a question I had asked myself a lot recently, but looking at Nimue, I realized a horrible truth. "It's not me that kills everything I come into contact with; it is you." I stood up. "It is you that has destroyed everything good in my life."

She scoffed. "I'm glad that you have such a high opinion of me, but if that's true, it's simply an inconsequential side effect of me living my life."

"Maybe, but I helped Hypnos destroy your plot to overthrow the Dream Realm."

"Again, not anything I planned. I just wanted to get back to Earth. Epiales's vendetta against Urgu was more Hypnos's problem than mine."

I balled my fists. "But you admit to letting him free knowing full well he would bring his wrath upon my people."

"They weren't your people!" Nimue shouted. "We were all trapped there, like ants in a farm. If you formed friendships in that place, you are more gullible than even I believed."

"You did not make friends because you are unlovable."

A flash of lightning shot down from the sky, and I rolled to avoid it. Nimue snapped her head up and watched a monster descend. The woman had no head, but a galaxy floated above her neck. "Thank you, Lydia, but I can handle one little girl."

The woman's voice echoed in my mind. "If that were true, then she would already be dead."

"I like to play with my food," Nimue growled with a sly smirk. "Perhaps to my detriment, but in this case, this one might be useful to our cause."

"I will never help you," I replied. "Except to die quickly."

I reached into my cape and flung two daggers in her direction. She raised an invisible barrier, and they stopped inches from her neck. She reached forward and plucked one out of the air, then jabbed it into my thigh.

"You only hurt yourself, being so stubborn," Nimue said. "This has always been a problem for you. Too hard-headed for your own good."

"I'll kill you!" I shouted, pulling the dagger from my thigh and watching pink magic work to congeal my blood and cover the wound. Whatever Nox had made me from, its power was increasing.

Nimue watched my leg heal. "Fascinating. And there's not a scratch left? This power is wasted on you. Why do you deserve such consideration while I am thrown to the wolves?"

So that was it. The true emotion Nimue had toward me was jealousy. I had been touched by Nox and given a second life for my service to Urgu, while Nimue was left to grovel for everything she got, making deals that took chunks of her soul.

"Because you are evil, Nimue, and I do not say that easily." With my leg healed, I stood up. "I like to think there is good even in the worst of us, but whatever good was once in you has been corrupted and rotten, so that your inside is even more hideous than your outside."

She lifted her hand to smite me but stopped herself. "Whatever we think of each other, we have the same enemy right now."

"The Spore?" I scoffed. "You think they are my enemy more so than you?"

Nimue narrowed her eyes. "If you do not believe so then you truly are myopic. What I have done to you is in the past. They are wounds that can heal, but what the Spore plan to do will destroy everything that you hold dear and warp the universe you know into something like me." She looked up at her vanguard. "Like us, and while I think we are beautiful, I know you don't want the universe to look like us."

"I do," Lydia whispered inside my head. I could see no hint of an expression, just the planets and stars dancing in the galaxy that circled where her face should be. "That would be a dream for me."

"And why wouldn't it be for you?" I asked. I couldn't help myself. My hatred for her was legendary, but so was my curiosity. "Why would you turn against the Spore?"

"I do not like being controlled," Nimue said. In that, I believed her. "The gods are horrible, but they are a known entity. Their cruelty is passe. They have no imagination, and they are predictable. They send pathetic humans like you to deal with their problems, while the Spore seems to have a more hands-on approach to control. I have only seen a glimmer of their cruelty, and I would much rather live in a universe controlled by the pitifully lazy than the ingeniously dogged. This creature planned for billions of years to bring back their family. The gods do not have that type of attention span."

"You think the universe will be easier to manipulate now, looking like that, then it will be with the Primordials?"

"I think that I—" She paused and looked at the others. "*We* are unique in this universe, and that makes us fearful. A million more like us, and we are less so, but in a nutshell, yes. It is easier to manipulate a fool, and the gods are certainly fools."

"I don't much like any of them."

A flaming woman that looked like she was made of pure fire spoke next. "Yes, that is right. We should destroy them all."

Nimue smiled. "One thing at a time, Cassandra. First, we destroy the Spore, then the gods will fall, in time."

"And then you will control the universe?"

Nimue shook her head. "No, then there will be chaos, and in the chaos, we will thrive."

I scratched my head. "I have to admit, that makes a ton of sense...but you must be out of your damned mind if you think I'm going to help you do anything."

Nimue smiled. "A pity."

She snapped her fingers and the three of them let loose

a barrage of attacks that sent me to my knees, screaming in pain. In the moments before I regained myself, Nimue bound me with a black rope, shoving me to the ground.

"We could have been great friends," she said before kicking me in the face. "In another life, maybe."

CHAPTER 32

ROSE

I pulled Blanche into the kitchen of a small rowhouse and asked her to sit down while I searched the bare cupboards for a snack. We had traversed most of the city, slowly and methodically over several hours.

"I'm tired," she said, clomping her front hooves as she rested her haunches on the ground.

"I know, sweetie." I sat down next to her and slid her a packet of graham crackers. "Eat these."

She bit into one. "They're gross."

"I know that, too." I crunched on a graham cracker anyway while I was thinking. Blanche was swift and quiet but having to account for her at all times made planning harder and caused me to take fewer risks than I would have on my own. *Perhaps that's for the best.* Maybe it was better to always think you had a child at your side to help you make better decisions. "I'm going to scout ahead."

The cruelty of the Spore was on full display throughout the city, as they picked up gods and mythical creatures alike, forcing them to join their cause. After what I had seen, I found it hard to believe there were any survivors left in the Celestial Realm besides the two of us, but people tended to be quite resourceful in the face of oppression. I made my way to the front window and peeked out. The street was empty.

"Rose," Blanche scream-whispered from the kitchen.

I whipped around just as a shadow loomed over her from the window. A god with thick horns and shaggy hair walked past. I could make out the visage through the slit between the thin drapes.

For a second, we stood still, thinking we'd been found, but then it moved on, the sound of footsteps making its way to the back door. I held out my hand and Blanche slid across the floor, careful to keep her hooves quiet on the marble floor. By the time she got to me, the god's hand was on the door. I yanked her through a small door under the stairs.

I pressed my hands onto our shoulders and cast a spell to make the shadows envelop us. We held our breath while the god clomped through the kitchen and pulled something out of the fridge. It gulped down a drink. When it was done it burped.

"These damn cursed bodies and their need to be fed."

It must not have been a god after all, as they could survive forever without eating, and only did so for the fun of it. Whatever stood in the kitchen was clearly a Spore host. I wrapped my hand around Blanche's mouth to prevent her from screaming.

I expected the monster to go back out the door, satis-fied, but they continued poking around the kitchen. Then I heard the crinkle of plastic. We had left the crackers on the table.

"Hrm," the monster growled. It turned and made its way down the hall. Its footsteps shook the little cave we had made for ourselves. We both nearly yelped out in fear, but I felt Blanche swallow her panic and I did the same.

The beast ripped open every door and pulled at every drawer upstairs before heading downstairs and ripping through the wall. I was sure we were caught. I readied a fireball as the monster moved closer again, but then there was another set of footsteps at the back door.

"Who—" Before the monster could finish its question, a small voice whispered something, and the monster crashed to the ground.

After a moment I heard the monster groan, and the small voice asked, "Are you okay?"

"What happened?"

"I will tell you soon, but first we must—"

Blanche couldn't hold it back anymore and a yelp escaped her lips.

The small voice spoke again. "One moment, please."

The door opened and a small halfling with big, bushy hair and bright blue eyes smiled at me. "Well, hello there. You can come out of the shadows now. I won't bite. I won't go so far as to say you're safe, but you're safe-ish, for now."

"Who are you?" I asked, my eyes darting between her and the minotaur that was rubbing its head.

"I'm Therigol," she replied. "And I'm happy to tell you more, but the Spore know we're here, and if we don't leave, like right now, we're all going to be gobbled up. And as my new friend can tell you, it's not pretty when that happens."

"No, it isn't," the minotaur groaned.

I wasn't sure I should believe her, but I had no other choice. If I didn't leave, the Spore would certainly find us, and I couldn't have that. "Lead the way."

CHAPTER 33
NIMUE

Idiot.

Red must have known that I would force her to help me if she denied me, so why did she insist on doing things the hard way? Had I really been that terrible to her? I supposed that I did depose her precious Ozma, and then I threw her off the ledge of my castle, but that was so long ago. Who could even remember it, let alone enough to hold it against me still?

Or was she still angry about the Fairy Realm? I hadn't even known she cared about that place until she attacked me on the battlefield.

"Hey," I said, kicking Red in the shin. "Wake up."

Her eyes fluttered open. She was still tied up, but I at least let her sit instead of laying her on the ground like an animal. I could be magnanimous. "What do you want?"

"I wanted to let you know that we stabilized your friend and fixed up his cart. See?" I gestured around the little room we were sitting in. "The wolves were a lost cause, but magic can do wonders to animate objects. I used it to gussy up the cart a bit. It was so drab in here. Isn't it nice now?" I gestured around us. "No, even I can't get over how boring it is to ride in a cart. The others chose to fly, but we have unfinished business, and I thought we could use some time to speak with each other. Why does it smell like cow dung? Did it always, even in the old days?"

"Probably, but nostalgia has made it seem better than it was." A smile crested across Red's face. "Admittedly, driving in a car is much better."

"Yes," I said, also smiling. "See, Gabrielle? We have much in common. How many people in the universe do you think have died, ended up in the Dream Realm, and then made their way back to the same planet, huh? Not very many, I would wager."

"I can only think of three off the top of my head: Rose, you, and me."

"That is my list as well." I nodded. "We are intrinsically linked, the three of us, in some sort of cosmic way."

"That sounds crazy," Red huffed.

I laughed. "Really? After all that has happened to us, you think that is crazy?"

"Everyone has a line, and mine is being linked to you in any way, except by your death."

"We are bound together whether you like it or not. After all, while Rose, you, and I, all saw the Fairy Realm together; only you and I have seen the Dark Planet, and the beauty contained here. We should be allies against the Spore, not enemies."

"Do you think I am so dumb as to believe you will turn against the Spore after they promised you incredible power?"

"Honestly?" I paused, waiting for her reply, but it never came. "I don't think you are dumb, but you are infinitely gullible, and I thought I could lie my way into your heart. I was thinking of lying to you even now to try and get you on my side. But there is one thing you value above everything else, and that is honesty. So here I am, cards on the table."

"This should be good. I have never seen you be honest in my whole existence. Very well, lay your cards out for me."

"I don't like the Spore, but they did offer me a powerful place in the new world order if we delivered you to them."

"That part I knew," I replied. "I have ears."

"Right. Well, since you know me so well, you might know that I am not beyond a double cross."

"Some might say it's the only thing you care about." Red shot me a look. "Being evil and all."

"I think ahead, and feel out which way the wind blows, and shift my allegiances accordingly." I shrugged. "You call that evil, but I call it practical."

"Practically evil in every way," she said. She truly was insufferable.

"I won't argue with you, Gabrielle," I said. "I come to offer you an olive branch. You hate me, and I nothing you. You have already tried to kill me, and you saw that it was quite impossible, so it is time to get over your petty grudge and work with me, or you will die."

"Why me?" Red asked. "Why do I have such a privilege as to be propositioned by you twice?"

"For one thing, and most importantly, you are here. Second, you are very tricky, and have evaded capture this long, which means you are capable. I'm surprised you are still alive, and yet, here you are, in my domain. It's annoying, but also shows how dogged you are. Third, the Spore want you for some reason, so that gives me leverage. And finally, there are few I can trust. They always end up dying on me, which is something I think we both have experience with."

"Yes, but mine generally die fighting against you, while I will bet you kill yours."

"Look who is being cruel now!" I put a hand on my chest. "Believe what you want, but many of my friends died trying to topple a cruel king to bring peace to this land, something that would have never happened if you had succeeded in stopping me before."

"I don't believe you. I'm sure any part you had in saving this land was simply an indirect result of your search for power."

I laughed. "I was actually about to walk away from the throne before you showed up. Now, I have returned to do what I must." I cleared my throat. "What has proved out again and again in my eons of life and death is that the only true power in the whole universe is just that—power. Either you wield it, or you bow to it. Even you, dear Gabrielle, bow to power."

"That is a lie."

"You bowed to Ozma once, who held the throne, and thus, power."

Red stiffened. "That is not why I bowed to her."

I shrugged. "Believe what you will, but I don't want to be ruled by the Spore any more than I wish to bow before the gods that rule over the universe now. So, I propose a truce, until we fulfill my plan. If you deny me now, I will not say another word about it and will deliver you like a lamb to slaughter. If you help me though, I believe we can change the universe for the better." I wasn't sure I believed my own words. "If you don't help me, the Primordials will attack, and I am very sure they will slaughter everyone in the Celestial Realm, and every realm they can find, along with every human in existence. Who knows? They might blow up the whole damned universe and start again from scratch."

Red bit her lip. "And if I help you, will my friends be safe?"

"That all depends on them. I have no desire to hunt them down, or anyone. I honestly do want peace—mostly for myself, but for the whole universe will be nice, too."

Red thought for a long moment, long enough to make me uncomfortable, but eventually she opened her mouth. "I have no other choice but to help you. I'm sure you know that."

"That depends on how stubborn you are and how tightly you hold to your virtues. If you want the least bloodshed, mine is the only option. If you hope to live, you will join me. Then again, you haven't ever seemed to value your life much."

"Very well then. I will help you, for now. The moment you show your true colors, though, I will bury a knife deep into your back."

"Then we have an accord, but you should know, many much better than you have tried to stick a knife in my back, and all have failed."

"It only takes once," Red replied. "That's the great thing about killing somebody."

"Silly, Red." I stood up. "You should know that nobody dies only once."

CHAPTER 34
ARIEL

I searched the ledger for every other mention of the sword, but there were too many, and none matched the description Hypnos gave me. None were engraved with "Hope Bringer" in Elvish, and after the last of my sanity left me, I fell down and cried. I hadn't even scoured five percent of Nox's vault. It would take me an eternity to go through the entire catalog, and even then, I might not find it.

I slogged out of the vault, dragging my feet, and flopped onto the bed Nox and Vivian shared. It smelled musty from disuse, and dust plumed from it when my body bounced on the springs. I coughed, but I didn't move for a long moment, letting the dust settle on my body and face. I knew what I had to do, but I didn't want to do it. There was only one person in Urgu that might know where the sword was…

Vivian.

Even then, it was a fool's errand. What were the odds that she shared an intimate moment where, in the throes of passion, they discussed the location of a sword that would save the fate of the Dream Realm? It was so illogical, but illogical was all I had to go on now as my hope of saving Urgu sunk further away.

I dove into the water and followed the tight tunnels until they expanded and combined into the cavern entrance. Four mermaids floated there, dressed in full battle regalia. I wasn't going toward them, though. I had no use for battle, and Nox's cavern had a secret tunnel into the depths of Urgu.

I turned towards the shadows. Nox sent a light into the darkness to guide travelers through the tunnels, and I had only known of her doing that once, to a red rider who held the fate of Urgu in her hands.

"*Urgu cor locate,*" I whispered. A light grew in my hands. I pushed it out into the sea, and it shot forward.

I took one last look at the berserkers ready to attack and followed the light. The circuitous piping was even more sinuous than it had been to get to Nox's secret vault, but eventually I rose into a small chamber containing a ladder that led toward a pink light.

I climbed up and up until it broke into a small ledge overlooking the whole of the Cavern of Dreams, where thousands, millions of dreams orbs filled an immense fissure. I heard tell of the cavern being nearly empty before Hypnos restarted the Heart of Urgu and allowed Dreamers back into his kingdom again.

The ledge led down to a small walkway, which followed around to a large door emblazoned with serpents, and further still an immense stairway that led up into the depths of the Obsidian Spindle.

Luckily, there was an elevator and I opted to conserve my energy and use it. It shot up to the surface quickly, causing my jaw to squeeze tight and my ears to pop. When the elevator dinged and the doors opened, Clotho and Lachesis were waiting for me at the base of the Spindle.

"We know what you are here for," Clotho said. "But we cannot allow you to open the Spindle and risk what we protect."

"I appreciate the care you take in this place, but if I don't get out there, then the whole of Urgu will be destroyed."

Lachesis closed her eyes. "We see what you need through the door, but it will lead to nothing but pain, ending with your untimely death."

"I have been dead once," I said, starting to move past them. "I don't fear it. I only fear the world ending due to my inaction."

"That is a noble sentiment," Clotho said. "But if the monsters get hold of the Spindle—"

"What?" I shouted. "What could possibly be worse than what is happening out there? Could the monsters get back to Earth without there being three of you? No." I squared my shoulders. "So, what do you really fear? Your own death? Because if you don't open that door, it will come by my hand, and not theirs."

I had been through the ringer, and I wasn't taking any resistance from anyone. I was running out of time, and I would get through that door, even if it killed me.

Lachesis dropped her head. "Very well."

She opened the door. I stepped out into a world on fire, and the door slammed behind me. Monsters had made their way onto the rainbow bridge, and the hydra that protected it was locked in battle with several of them—and winning, for the moment.

Standing atop the bridge, I felt the breadth of my power. When I stepped forward, I found myself on the other side of the bridge. I had teleported, something I had never been able to do before. I followed the walkway around to a door that was under attack from a half dozen hideous, misshapen monsters. I reached out my hand and lifted them into the air, sending them flying over the edge of the castle into the water below.

I pounded on the door. "Please, open up. It's Ariel. I'm not a monster. I need to get inside now. It's urgent."

There was nothing for a moment, but then the doors opened and Lady Lynx peered out. "My gods, it really is you. How—"

"We don't have time. I need to get to Hypnos's dungeon right now."

She cocked her head but didn't question me. She turned and led me through the castle as the Emerald guards barricaded the doors. I had never seen golems made of emerald before, but they had molded themselves from the flawless gems of the castle and taken up protecting the building. There were hundreds of them mixed in with the souls guarding the hallways.

"We expected you sooner. When the monsters came, we assumed your quest was folly."

I shook my head. "No, it was not folly. It was Nox, taken over by a monster, who ripped open the holes to the Nightmare Realm. She aims to weaken the barrier between our world and the universe at large, so that when her family invades, they can take it over. Hypnos sent me to find a way to save all of Urgu, but I need my sister's help to find what I need."

"Oh my," Lady Lynx said. "Well, if you need her help, I

fear we are very much doomed. She has not been helpful, or forthcoming since her imprisonment."

I smiled. "I have a way of getting under her skin."

"Let us hope so," Lady Lynx said, pushing open a door to a rush of hot air. "She is below. May the gods be with you."

CHAPTER 35

CHELLE

"Drop her there," I said to Hypnos when we reached a large, vertical grate at the end of the duct system. We'd found a way up into the building's sewer system and had been snaking through them, sometimes having to backtrack, looking for a way out. Hypnos carried Ariel the whole time, complaining about it to no end. I had no sympathy for him, though, because he was a god, and they all sucked, especially him.

"That feels so much better," he replied, cracking his back. "She's not heavy, but she's not light either."

Through the grate, I saw a city sprawling out as the water surged out into a waterfall under us. "Looks like we finally found a way out."

"About time."

"*Fragore*," I shouted, and the huge grate crunched in on itself and fell down the hundred foot drop down to the water below. "Okay, bring her over here."

Hypnos huffed and puffed. When he joined me, he gulped as he looked down. "Far fall."

"You're a god, man. Sack up."

He grabbed my hand and nodded. Together we dropped off the edge. The water under the building flew toward us faster and faster...until suddenly it didn't. We were suspended in the air for a second, and then instead of descending, we flew upwards.

"What's happening?" Hypnos shouted, kicking his feet in the air until we were above the grate. We soared toward a platform at the base of the domed building.

"I don't know, but—" I turned to see Nox above us, leaning over the platform, shaking her head. "Well, noodles."

Hovering in the air above her were enough gods to blot out the stars. They were still, simply looking out onto the horizon.

"Well, aren't you all very clever," Nox said, and she placed us down on the platform. Two dozen gods surrounded her in a semicircle. "Did you think I wouldn't have safeguards in place just in case you happened to escape?"

"I didn't think about it much," I replied, staring at her and trying to contain my fear.

"And now?" She turned to Hypnos.

"To be completely honest," he answered, "we're a little freaked out."

"He's freaked out, I'm more miffed," I countered.

Nox turned her head, studying Ariel's sleeping form. "And I see you've sent her into the Dream Realm. Do you really think that silly sword will help you?"

"It was a safeguard you—my mother put in place just in case anyone found a way to breach our defenses, and we were all incapacitated."

Nox tapped her head. "It's too bad only I know where it is, and I'm not telling."

"She'll find it. I have faith in her."

Nox smiled. "Before I kill her, though? The clock is ticking. All the pieces are just about to fall into place."

She pointed behind her. The Obsidian Spindle rose high into the air, cutting an imposing image onto an already imposing situation. It didn't take long before a large white door cut into the Spindle and five figures exited, the one in the center carrying another. They were twisted versions of women, turned into monsters, each more deranged than the last, but I recognized the one in the center, tied up, bound, and barely hanging on to consciousness.

Red.

"Let her go!" I screamed, rushing forward, but Nox's magic held me back.

The one behind Red chuckled. "Chelle? Well, isn't this a surprise. You have really chosen the most annoying beings as your vessels, haven't you, Nox."

Her voice was familiar, but I didn't recognize her face. Her white skin had been shattered like glass, and small bright lights ran through her skin. The black cracks in her skin continued up to her face, and it looked as though black tears ran down the sides of her cheeks and pooled around her chin.

"I did not choose them, Nimue." Nox replied, and I saw blood. "I would have chosen more malleable hosts."

"Nimue!" I screamed. "Of course you would be in league with the Spore."

"Oh, hush," Nimue replied. "You make it seem so lurid. They made me an offer I absolutely had to accept, and I did so. That's your problem, Gorgon. You always fight against entropy, but I have found it's best to succumb to it. More fun, too."

"Is that what you call being a ruthless, blood-hungry tyrant?"

"Please," Nimue replied. "You flatter me."

"Do you have her?" Nox asked. "Or is that a vole you have caught to show me?"

Nimue threw Red down and she slid across the floor with a squeaky thud. "That's her. It cost us a pretty penny to find her, too."

Nox kicked Red and smiled, looking at Nimue. "You have done well. You will have a treasured seat in the new world order."

"About that," Nimue said. "I was hoping to get started destroying the old world order right about now. There are about a million gods I would very much like to obliterate, if you'll let me. I have a lot of rage."

Nox laughed. "I'm using most of them now, but there are still some stragglers in town. Feel free to destroy anything you find. Consider it the first part of your reward, but do not disturb me until the ritual is finished."

Nimue smiled. I could only tell because her white teeth shone like pearls. "I wouldn't dream of it. After all, I am very anxious to meet our new overlords."

"All of us are," Nox replied, before turning to me. "Well, most of us."

Their cackles turned my bones, and I wanted nothing more than to slice their throats. But in that moment, I felt very small, like all hope was lost. I only had one wish: to see Rose one more time before I died. It was a selfish wish since that would mean she'd been captured, too, but the heart was not logical. The only thing I wanted was to be consoled, because I was very sure that I was about to die, for good this time.

And I doubted Rose would save me, no matter how much she tried to. After all, we were fighting against entropy.

CHAPTER 36

ARIEL

I never wanted to see Vivian again. Not after what she did to me, but I couldn't deny that I loved her. You can't help who you love, but you can help their access to you. I appreciated that Hypnos had locked her away in a deep, dark dungeon so that I would never have to see her again... except now that was exactly where I was going.

The slick, stone stairs echoed as I descended into the dank dungeon. When I finally reached the bottom, I was met with the smell of moldy bread and wet towels. The ground had been flooded recently; the water having receded to small puddles throughout the room. There was no way this was unintentional. The Dream Realm bent to Hypnos's every command.

"Sister," Vivian hissed. I turned toward a dark cell. Her voice was almost too weak to have an emotion, and hoarse like she had walked the entire Sandlands without a bit of water. She had seen me before I saw her, and when I laid eyes on her it was only a pair of bright yellow eyes that peered out, lighting the rest of her body with a faint glow. "I didn't expect to ever see you again."

My eyes adjusted to the dim light. Vivian had changed much since our last meeting. Her skin was dry and blotchy. It flaked off onto the ground, and there was a small pile of it on the ground, and wisps around the cell floor.

"It's good to...I am hap— You look..." I couldn't find the right words. It was not good to see her, I was not happy, and she did not look well. She looked pathetic, and it brought a small amount of joy to my heart. "How are you?"

She opened her arms. "How does anyone look when they are being tortured?"

"I don't believe that is what's happening to you, is it?"

"What else would you call it?" She picked a piece of dry skin off her flaking body. "You know my skin dries on land after a time, and Hypnos keeps the water away until I am close to death. Why would he do that, if not to punish me?"

I had never thought about a mermaid on dry land. I thought the thing keeping them in the water was that their fins didn't work well on land, and they did not like feeling helpless.

"I'm sure if I spoke to him, he would have a perfectly reasonable explanation for all this," I replied. "The thing is—"

"It would be just like you to think of the best in everyone. It is your most annoying trait."

"I know you think that, but—"

"It nearly got you killed in Nox's vault, and yet you still choose to believe in the good in me, don't you? Can nothing damage that horrible spirit of yours?"

If the end of the universe and my imminent death couldn't do it, I very much doubted a few harsh barbs from my sister would do the trick, but she did have a way of getting under my skin.

"Not that I can think of," I said. "Sorry to disappoint you."

"That is not what disappoints me about you. That list is too long to mention."

I stomped my foot. "I'm not here for your pettiness. I have real problems that require immediate solutions."

Vivian coughed. "I'm sorry my suffering isn't real enough for you."

"That's not what I meant."

"No, please. What could the great Ariel need from me today?" There was venom on each syllable.

Was I really so desperate to ask for her help? Before I could answer myself, the words fell from my mouth. "You don't have to say it like that, but—" I sighed and held out my hands. "Did Nox ever talk to you about a sword engraved with the words 'Hope Bringer' in Elvish?"

"Oh, what a favor you ask." Vivian studied me. "How important is it to you?"

"No less than the fate of the universe rests in the balance," I replied, sternly.

"Yes, but how much does it matter to you, personally?"

"As a resident of this universe, it matters very much. How much does it matter to you?"

She leaned forward and whispered harshly. "Not a lot, since if the universe is over, my punishment would be, too." Her eyes lit up. "Yes, the end of the universe actually sounds quite nice."

I crossed my arms. "I knew this was a mistake."

"I know where it is," she said, matter of fact. "The sword I mean, and I'll show it to you, for a price."

"And what price is that?"

She squeezed the bars tightly. "Freedom."

"Hypnos would never—"

"He's not here, and that tells me he's in trouble, too. Come on, I'm one bratty little girl. Do you really think my punishment is worth the end of the universe?"

I nearly did. "No, I suppose not, but I don't think I can."

She shrugged. "You cannot find it without me. Nox kept it hidden somewhere safe and only revealed it to me in the most intimate of moments. I'm not sure she even remembers she did so, frankly, but it has consumed my thoughts since."

"If you lead me on a wild goose chase," I replied, stepping closer to her. "I swear to the gods..."

She laughed, pulling herself close to the bars until her face pressed against them. "You'll what, kill me? I already told you that would be preferable to all this."

I wanted so badly to dust her, and I was sure she was planning to betray me. I couldn't risk the end of the universe, though, even if she never deserved to see the light of day again.

"Are you sure you know where it is? Because if you don't—"

"Once again, what could you possibly do to me?"

"Gods damn it stop interrupting me, and yes, I will dust you where you stand."

She laughed. "That'll be the day, princess, but ask yourself this...how can I hurt you in this state?"

She wasn't wrong. She was barely able to move. I glared at her and asked, "Where is the key to your cell?"

"Hypnos's word opened and closed the door. You were blessed by him, so it should be all you need. Just press your hand on the bar and say '*patefacio sursum.*' Easy as that."

Every alarm bell in my head went off at once, but I had no other choice. I did as she said, and a jolt shook through me as the cell snapped open. Vivian muttered the spell to turn her fins into legs. When she had transformed, she ambled out of the cell. She knelt down and slurped up water from a puddle before laying down and rolling in it, soaking up every spare drop.

When she was done, she stood up, and while she didn't look well, she certainly looked better.

"That was refreshing," she said with a smirk, walking toward the stairs. "Come now. Wouldn't want to disappoint your boss."

"He's not my—" I growled. "You are so infuriating. Just march, okay?"

"Whatever you say, sis."

CHAPTER 37
ROSE

"We're actually going the other way," I said after Therigol led us a few blocks in the opposite direction from Rama's mansion. My legs felt weak, but I was getting stronger. "So, if you'll excuse us—"

I grabbed Blanche and turned in the other direction, but Therigol grabbed my arm. "You don't want to go back that way. The Spore are even thicker there. Only one place in the whole city is safe enough right now. You follow me, or you become one of them."

I didn't know if she was telling the truth, but she wasn't a Spore, and she seemed to know who they were, so I decided to let up and follow her. After all, we were looking for sanctuary and a way to end the Spore, and Therigol seemed to have a bead on both.

"Fine," I replied. "But can you please let go of me."

"Gladly."

She dropped my arm and led us into a sewer grate on the edge of the city. We traveled through a series of tunnels that got worse and worse smelling the further we walked. I always imagined gods vaporizing their waste, but it seemed they had the same disgusting bowels as the rest of us.

"How did you save me?" the minotaur asked, still rubbing his fuzzy head. "I don't remember anything from the time those spores—it was terrible. I could see out of my eyes, but everything was hard to hear and slow, like being underwater in a pool."

Therigol held up a squirt gun, like the Super Soakers I used when I was a kid, but with a bigger barrel for water, and it glowed brightly as she brought it into the dim light. The glow was the same blue color as the spores that Kadlu gave me, except here there were also flecks of red and orange in it.

"I hit you with this," she said. "One squirt directly into your mouth leeches the spores out of you, and then I banish them to another dimension, or something." She pulled out a small yellow box covered with runes.

"Who showed you how to do this?" I said softly.

"She used to be a maid at one of the mansions. Her name is—"

"Maricel?" I asked hopefully. I remembered that Maricel had done a spell to scatter the Spore back when we rescued Rama. Perhaps she had made it back here and was alive...it was too wonderful a thing to dream.

Therigol nodded. "That's right. She came here with a ton of this pollen, and a plan. Once we saw what she could do, we all signed up to help. Only problem is that for every one we save, they take three. We barely have anyone left, which is why I'm sure glad I found you three."

My heart was aflutter as we continued, but when the tunnels finally emptied in front of a big mansion, all of that nearly vanished. The word "Odinson" was written in large, gold letters across the portico, and the statue over the fountain told me exactly who once lived there.

"You're squatting at Odin's house?" I asked. "Are you mad? He's a Spore!"

"No, he was a Spore, but he died, and so did his wife, which makes this perfect. Nobody looks for us here because they think everyone is dead."

I didn't like the idea of going inside the house that once trapped my beloved Chelle, but it was a far cry better than standing out in the open like an idiot. I followed Therigol through the door and into a large kitchen, where a dozen gnomes and a golem wearing a tuxedo were busy at work filling more water guns with their concoction.

"Ovli, have you—" Maricel walked into the room and stopped when she saw my face. She rushed forward and wrapped her arms around me. "You're alive!"

"You're alive, too. How did you end up here?"

Maricel let go of me. "The Spore redirected all Spindles to the Celestial Realm to make it easier to round up the gods. I tried to take several and still kept ending back here, so I decided to help the only way I knew how."

"That's smart, but why was the station abandoned?"

"It wasn't when I got here. They must have grown tired of waiting for more people. Maybe that means the end is here." She looked outside through the window. "No, I don't see a beacon."

"What beacon?" I asked.

Maricel turned from the window. "The Spore, they are creating a weapon of incredible energy to rip a hole in the universe. That's going to take a lot of power, and a ton of energy. It's going to light up the sky when it goes off li—"

"Like a beacon," Blanche said.

"That's right, cutie," Maricel said. "And who are you?"

I spoke up when Blanche shied away. "Her dad was captured by the Spore. I found her and am helping her find a safe place."

Maricel smiled at the girl. "We're going to get your father back, okay?"

"Okay," Blanche said, but she was unenthusiastic.

"Would you like some pizza?" Maricel snapped her fingers when Blanche nodded and spoke to one of the gnomes. "Can you bring this girl into the parlor and get her some pizza?"

"Sure," the gnome growled. "I guess I'm fine just being a servant again. Come on, girl."

"You're not a servant. You're helping a friend."

The gnome smiled and bowed his head slightly. "Of course, ma'am."

When Blanche was gone, I looked at Maricel. "You shouldn't lie to the girl."

"I'm not lying. We're going to get them all back."

"How? By spraying them with water?"

She paced. "When that beacon goes off, every one of my troops stationed around the city will rush the spire on top of the mountain. With any luck, that will draw the Spore-controlled gods out of hiding to deal with the threat. Once we draw as many of them as possible, that's when I'm going to unleash a thunderstorm down upon them to try to free our brethren."

"You're going to drench them all with the counteragent, aren't you?" I laughed. "It's kind of brilliant."

"The Spore would smell it a mile away usually, and run to hide, but they can't while the beacon is lit. They need every one of their gods protecting that stupid tower. It's a big risk, but it's the one chance we have. If the Spore succeed—"

"They won't," I said, looking out at the tower.

"I appreciate your confidence, but they certainly have the upper hand right now."

"They always do, right before they get taken down. Trust me, this isn't my first time."

"I hope you're right," Maricel said, joining me at the window. "I really don't want the universe to end."

"All we can do is fight like hell to make sure that doesn't happen and believe in hope even when it's stupid to do so."

She smiled. "That I can do."

CHAPTER 38

RED

The Spore gods threw Chelle and me into a sterile room with smooth metal walls, bound tightly so that we could barely move. "And don't try to use magic, either," Nox said. "It's warded, obviously."

"Great," Chelle grunted after Nox closed the door. "What are we going to do now?"

I shrugged and said the only thing I was told to say. "I'm sure it will all be okay."

I didn't like Nimue, but I loved espionage. The chance to use those skills to destroy the Spore was too delicious for words. The first rule of spy craft was that you didn't tell everyone in the world about what you were trying to do. Not only could they blab, or try to help and risk getting themselves hurt, but if the room was bugged, like any good prison would be, then your plot was bound to be overheard. No, even to an old friend, all you could do was smile, nod, and do what you were told.

Nimue knew monsters like the Spore better than I did, so I decided to defer to her judgement, even though it made my skin crawl. I looked down at my wrist. Nimue had carved a glyph into it older than time itself, one that would banish the Spore, but I had to get close enough to Nox to grab her. If I did, then I could destroy the infestation and rid the goddess of the Spore, and send a sickness through the whole organism, giving us a chance to escape before Nimue blew the whole building sky high.

That explosion would ignite a chain reaction that would quake through the whole of the Celestial Realm, rending it a hundred ways and turning it inhabitable. What would happen then? I thought to ask, but she was too focused on her plan. With people like that, it was better to just point them at a nail and allow them to be the hammer. I had enough on my plate destroying the Spore, let alone fighting Nimue as well. No, better to separate them, turning them against each other, and then by the time the dust settled, I would bury a dagger into her spine and watch her bleed out on the ground, drowning in her own blood.

It was morbid, but then, I was a killer.

"What the hell is that supposed to mean, Red?" Chelle scoffed. "We're in a prison in the Celestial Realm, waiting to have our souls used to power an intergalactic laser. What do you mean, you think it will all be okay? State your evidence, because from where I'm sitting—tied up, mind you—nothing is going to be okay, ever again."

"Things are not always as they seem."

"You suck. When did you start sucking?"

"I think I kind of always sucked," I replied, flatly. It was the truth, too.

"You know what. It doesn't matter." Chelle slid down to the floor. "What do you think they're doing with Hypnos?"

"I don't know. I assume they will use him as a conduit for his mother's power until he explodes."

"You said that so matter of fact—are you a serial killer?"

I chuckled. "Probably, given that I've killed many, many people across vast horizons and on multiple planets, and that I don't feel bad about it. So yes, I am a psychopath."

"Wow," she replied. "I always say it doesn't matter, but I always feel something when I kill somebody, even if it's not much."

"Well," I dropped to the floor with a groan. "You're a lot younger than me...though I hope it never happens to you. It's probably why I'm so good at hunting monsters, because at heart, I am one."

"No, no, no," Chelle replied. "Don't say that...you are not very good at hunting monsters."

"Excuse me? I literally tracked Nimue from Earth to the Dark Planet."

"Yeah, and what happened after that? She cleaned your clock." Chelle smiled. "Relax, Red. I'm messing with you."

"Oh," I replied. "It doesn't happen to me often."

"Oh I know. I've known you long enough." She paused, and I felt the conversation turn. "Have you seen Rose?"

"Not for a while—not since Rama's house, before I came to see you."

"Crap. I hope she's okay. I would never forgive myself if something happened to her." Chelle buried her face in her knees. "I wish she never met me."

"No." I rolled toward her. "You don't mean that."

"I do. If she never met me, she never would have learned about monsters, and she never would have—"

"Fallen into the Dream Realm? Yes, she would have, and she wouldn't have known anything when she got there. You gave her that, Chelle. You're the reason she survived at all."

"No," Chelle looked back at me. "You would have saved her if I didn't. This is all my fault."

Tears started falling down her face and I had no idea what to do. "I'm not equipped for this kind of thing."

"Me either," she blubbered. "This sucks. This so much more than sucks, but I'm about to die and I can't seem to come up with a better word."

I was next to her now, and I pushed my face close so her eyes met mine. "We are not going to die. Do you understand me?"

Chelle's eyes narrowed. "You are so confident."

"And you are so dense," I growled. "Just trust me, okay? I know I'm not as close to you as I am to Rose, but we've been through a lot together. Remember when you saved my life with Zabasha?"

She grinned. "That was some fight."

"And I owe you a life debt. I aim to pay it today." My eyes never wavered from hers. "Do you trust me?"

Chelle didn't hesitate. "Yes, I do."

"Then, trust me when I tell you that we are not going to die."

It was then that the doors opened, and two guards rushed in, dragging us out into the cold of the hallway, to oblivion. I regretted asking Chelle to trust me, because I wasn't sure I could deliver.

CHAPTER 39
NIMUE

"What is your plan here, my dear?" Lydia whispered into my head. From the way she talked to me, calmly and with none of her usual stomach-dropping tone, I got the distinct impression that she was only talking to me, and not Delilah or Cassandra.

"Chaos," I replied, landing in the center of an abandoned street. "Nothing but utter and complete chaos."

"I'm all for that," Delilah said, landing next to me. "But if you plan to destroy the Celestial Realm, then we'll need some powerful magic, and I've never learned anything that can destroy a whole planet. If I had, I would have used it already."

"Me too." Cassandra nodded along with her sisters. "I would have blown up a galaxy to rid myself of Hastur."

"There is a way, I assure you." I tapped my chest. "Baba kept a journal of all the dark magic she ever learned, along with how to destroy all her enemies. One of them is a spell that can not only rip the Spore from their hosts but eliminate them forever. The only problem with it is that the sonic blast required will destroy everything within a hundred miles of the blast."

"That's a big blast, but it's not earth shattering."

I pulled the journal out of my cape, and it sprung open. Elvira's voice spoke wistfully through it. "You're right about that, sister."

"Elvira?" Cassandra asked. "How did you—"

"No time," Elvira said. "Every minute is critical, but just know it is very nice to be in your presence again."

"I assume you have a plan, then?" I asked.

"I do. I have been going over the text since I bonded with this book. By my estimations, we'll need two dozen glyphs strategically placed around the city to cover the entirety of the Celestial Realm, and if we activate them all at the same time, I am confident it will rock this realm to its foundation."

"May I see this glyph?" Cassandra asked. The diary flipped to the complex glyph I had carved into Gabrielle's arm. Cassandra studied the page for a long time. "I believe I know how to modify this glyph so the spell has half the range horizontally, but double the penetration vertically, so that it can bore even deeper into the core of the planet."

"What does that mean?" I asked.

She looked over at me. "If we arrange twelve glyphs around the Celestial Realm, clustered mostly around the Oracle, then I think we can destroy the whole of this accursed place, and the Spore along with it."

"That sounds lovely," I replied, a big smile on my face. "Then, let's get started."

CHAPTER 40
CHELLE

We were going to die, and if Red thought otherwise she was a fool. We were trapped; bound in the arms of gods who were leading us to our deaths. They would use us to open a gate to another universe and unleash untold horrors on the universe. My attempt to do good was for naught, and all that good I'd tried to stack up would be nothing compared to the evil I unwittingly helped set free.

"There you are," Nox said with a booming voice as we entered the circular room we'd just escaped from. We had been so close to freedom.

An enormous laser at the top of the dome pointed up to the heavens, and originated several feet above the ground, where a giant altar was erected.

In the center of the altar, Hypnos has been strapped down, his four extremities pulled tight. They each abutted a metal bed. Ariel laid on one, her hands stretched out above her, so that her left index finger touched Hypnos' right hand.

"So, what?" I asked. "Hypnos is a conduit between us or something?"

Nox smiled. "That's correct, though it wasn't very hard to surmise. Even a mortal, like you, could figure it out without much prompting."

"I'm not really a mortal, though, am I? Otherwise, I wouldn't be here."

She shrugged. "You think like a mortal. Tie them down on the beds. If they give you any trouble, knock them out."

The gods guarding us untied our bindings. I struggled and fought against them, pushing them away from me. I reasoned that if the Spore's plan relied on magic, then it meant this room wasn't guarded against it.

"*Metallum stamine!*" I shouted, but nothing happened.

"Fool, this is platinum," one of the guards said, shoving me down. "You can't bend it through silly tricks. Only a god has that kind of power."

"*Turbo!*" A large tornado formed, lifting two of the guards high into the sky, but Nox cut through it, and the gods fell back to the ground. A second later, they rose like nothing had happened, and without so much as a dent on the metal ground, despite the sizeable fall.

Red rushed behind Nox and tried to wrap her in a bear hug, but the goddess broke out of it quickly and painlessly, sending Red sliding across the room.

"Are you okay?" I called to her as she tried to right herself.

"Anything but," Red moaned. "It's good to fight with you again, though I wish I had that golden dagger I lent you. Don't suppose you have it around, do you?"

"Sorry, but I lost it in the fight I lost with Nox. I think Rose has it now."

"Oh, good. Well, I hope she's on her way to save us."

The three gods closed in on me. "Me too, cuz it doesn't look good."

One of the guards lunged and I fired a blast of water, sending them flying backwards. I used the water like a whip to crack the other nameless god in the head, cutting a small gash on their cheek that healed almost immediately.

"Enough of this." Nox snapped her fingers and a dozen more guards spilled into the room, each of them powerful gods like the ones I could barely touch, let alone hurt. Nox said what I was thinking: "You can't possibly win."

"We don't have to win," I replied. "You just have to lose. *Ignis!*"

I shot the biggest fireball I could create, and it exploded directly beneath the laser. It was my best attempt to try to send it crashing to the ground and end the Spore's plan once and for all. When the smoke cleared though, there was no damage to the device. Not even my most powerful spell could touch the enormous device.

Nox tsked. "When will you learn that you can't stop the inevitable?"

There was only one option left, and I was loath to take it, but...*Goodbye, Rose.* If I was going out, I was going out on my terms. I placed my hands on my own heart and channeled as much energy I could manage into creating an explosion in my own body. If I truly was made of magic, then it should be enough to destroy the whole building, and everything inside of it. *I'm sorry, but it's for the best.*

"*Infernalis calor.*" I felt my body heat up as a tear fell down my face. My hands and feet went up, and then my arms and legs, until I was one ball of molten fire. I should have burnt through myself, but instead, I just stood there, slightly uncomfortable, like being in Phoenix midday, during the summer, but it was nothing my body couldn't handle. I smashed my hands into myself and tried to say the spell again, but to no greater effect. I tried a third time, and nothing happened.

"You idiot," Nox said, walking toward me. "Your body is a generator for power, but like any other generator, you need to know how to access and wield that power. You are nothing but a dumb human. Do you really think you could possibly understand how to wield the power of the gods?"

"You can shut up now," Red growled, latching onto Nox from behind and squeezing her tightly. "*Infernale spolium, ad ima unde venisti, deleo!*"

I had never seen Red create a spell before, but her dictation was perfect, as was her pronunciation. As she spoke, her arm began to glow a brilliant orange, and that orange transferred over to Nox, who shrieked as a bolt of energy shot from her a hundred feet into the air and exploded above the planetarium like a brilliant firework.

When it was done, Nox fell to the floor in a smoking heap. Red rolled off her, her face and arm charred black like she had covered herself in molten rock. "Did it work?"

I looked over to Nox. Her eyes were no longer black, but the brilliant purple I remembered. "What happened? Chelle? Red? Wha—" She looked around as a dozen guards descended on us. "Well, this isn't how I expected this to go."

"What do you mean?" I said. "Were you planning this? Were you working with the Spore this whole time?"

"No," Nox said. "Of course not, but can we escape first, and then I can explain later?"

"It better be a doozy of an explanation," Red said, coughing black bile. "Otherwise, I'm going to kill you."

Nox's eyes ping-ponged between the dozens of Spore gods converging upon us. "You can have at it if they don't beat you to it."

CHAPTER 41
ROSE

Maricel, the other refugees, and I were eating dinner at Odin's mansion, soberly and quietly. I had eaten enough to regain my strength and was getting antsy to attack the Spore and save Chelle. The table shook when a huge light shot up in the distance and exploded.

"Is that it?" I asked.

We'd been waiting for the laser blast that would cut a hole in the very fabric of existence and unleash untold horrors onto the universe—

Except that this explosion wasn't a consistent blast, not a continuous beam, not a singular explosion. The position was right, but the duration was all wrong.

Maricel looked out the window with me. "I don't think it's what we're looking for, but the others are going to see it as such, so we have no choice but to attack now."

"And what if you're wrong and the others don't join us?"

She grinned. "Then this will be the shortest attack in history."

I studied the golden dagger in my hand while Maricel

whistled and walked to the door. She threw a pair of swords to a half-elf as the gnomes cooking in the kitchen grabbed knives from the range and made their way to the door. It was then I realized that every single being in the mansion would be fodder for the attack. None would be spared not even...

...Blanche.

I sprinted through the horde rushing toward the door until they thinned, and it broke open to a small alcove filled with priceless artifacts. There, in the center, Blanche stood shaking, staring down at a silver machete. She looked over at me, tears streaming down her face.

"I...I can't..." she muttered as I wrapped her in a hug. "Please don't make me."

"It's okay, baby girl," I whispered. "You don't have to fight if you don't want to."

"Yes, she does," Maricel said. "We need everyone if we have any hope of winning."

Blood boiled inside of me. I broke from Blanche and approached Maricel, hoping to intimidate her. "She's a child."

"So what?" Maricel replied. "She's a body, and we need everybody we can spare."

"We came here for safety."

"And we gave it to you, but freedom doesn't come free. Now, it's time to fight for it."

I pointed back to the child. "She's not fighting—"

"She'll do as she's told if she wants to get her father back." Maricel's voice was flat, dead, like all the heart had drained from it.

"What's that supposed to mean?"

"It means we all lost somebody—" She bit her lip. "Some more than others. Blanche has a chance to see her father again, but we need her help to make it possible. If she doesn't join us, then others will falter, and it will all fall apart."

"She's just a kid—"

"Half the people here are kids that made it here without their families, and the rest have been cast away, too pathetic for even the Spore to bother with. We are the last hope for my people, and for hers."

Before I could continue arguing, a small hand grabbed my arm. I turned back to see Blanche, her lip quivering but her resolve sturdy, wiping her eyes with the hand that held the dagger. "It's okay. I can do it."

"You don't have to fight." I knelt down to her level. "I can keep—"

"I want to." She bit the edge of her lip and her eyes narrowed in determination. "I wanna get my dad back."

"That's a very brave decision, Blanche," Maricel said.

"Are you sure?" I asked, one last time in my most comforting voice. She nodded and I reached out her hand. "Okay. I'll protect you as best I can."

Maricel held the door as I led Blanche into the main foyer. I saw then what Maricel meant. I never saw the naivete in the eyes of the others before, or maybe their youth shone through their fear, but at least half were school-aged, and probably more. The others hadn't held a weapon before. Their hands shook as they clung to their weapons.

They looked at us for guidance, and when we rejoined the fold, the fear washed away, and resolve replaced it just like it had for young Blanche. My heart broke for them, but a part of me knew that Maricel was right. We needed bodies to succeed in this, even if they would be little more than cannon fodder. It was moments like this that I was grateful to no longer be the queen of Oz.

Maricel climbed onto a table, and everyone huddled around her. She was little more than a maid, and yet she held the rapt attention of everyone in the great hall, including me.

"Today we fight the last battle for our freedom. If we lose, the whole universe loses, so leave it all out there." A person bumped into me, and I looked down to find a water gun filled with blue liquid and flecks of red being held up by tiny hands. "Remember to shoot for the mouth, and to conserve your ammo, since there is no more of this stuff. Don't shoot until you see the whites of their black, cold eyes. I know that's dangerous, but once your bottles are empty, then you will be defenseless."

I grabbed two bottles from the tiny hands of the artilleryman and turned to Blanche. "Here, take these."

I handed her my gun and my reserve cartridges. "No, I can't—"

"Trust me. I'll be okay." I made a tiny blue flame in my hand. "Trust me, okay?"

"Okay," she whispered.

I wanted to tell her she would be okay, but I didn't know if that was true. There was every possibility that despite my best efforts, she would die on the battlefield.

Maricel hopped down from the table. It wasn't a great speech, or even barely a serviceable one, but the recruits were fired up all the same. She opened the door and held up her water gun. The others did the same.

"To victory, and to the death of the Spore!"

Everyone shouted as they rushed out the door into the darkness of the Celestial Realm.

CHAPTER 42

RED

That was a big, bad stupid idea. Nimue thought that taking out Nox would disrupt the collective, but instead the more than twenty gods surrounding us were laser-focused on us, sizing us up with their black eyes.

"So," they said in unison. "Nimue has betrayed me."

"How do you—"

"Yes," the Spore continued after a moment's thought and contemplation, as if it was analyzing a million scenarios at once across its network of brains. "Yes, that is the only explanation that makes sense here. No matter. She thinks she holds the power here, but she will soon find the truth of the matter."

"She always did think she was too big for her britches," Nox growled under her breath. "Any ideas how to get out of this?"

"You just saw my best plan," I replied. I looked down at my charred, mangled hands. "And now I think I'm useless in a fight."

"And you, Gorgon?" Nox asked Chelle.

"Fight like hell and hope we don't die?"

"Brilliant." Nox sighed. "Then I suppose it is up to me."

She clapped her hands and sent out a giant tremor. The gods rose in the air to avoid the seismic activity. I thought she had made a miscalculation, but as they rose in the air, she shot a giant ball of air, smashing them into the walls. She wasn't done yet. She pulled her hands together, and shadows came to her aid to hold the gods in place.

"That won't stop them for long," Nox said. She took both of us in one hand and shot up into the air. I wanted to care about the poor girl we left lying unconscious on the table, but I couldn't gather the energy. I felt guilty about leaving Hypnos, but he was a god, and his death was not integral to the Spore's plan.

"You're just going to leave your son down there?" Chelle asked. "That's cold-blooded."

"If I don't, then the whole of the universe is doomed."

"You don't have to convince us," I said. "He can handle himself. I'm sure Hypnos will be fine."

"I'm not so sure as that," Nox said with some trepidation. "But I have no other choice."

She stayed close to the laser until we shot out of the top of the domed ceiling. I hoped for salvation, but there was little hope even when we escaped. Instead, I looked out in horror as a thousand gods circled the dome and closed rank around us.

"Did you really think you could escape?" the Spore said in unison, their voices booming in my head and causing my whole body to tremble. "We have had an eternity to plan for this moment."

Nox shuddered. Then, she tensed again as her strength coalesced inside of her, and she raced toward the lightest concentration of gods. As she moved, a dozen fireballs molded around her, and an arc of flame shot out in front of her. From the darkness created by the light, the gods' shadows pulled from their masters and began to attack them.

She flung fireballs and they found their targets. For one merciful second, I thought we would break through, but that was before a big gust of air blew out the fire and the shadows dissipated. With that, the gods overcame their attackers and turned to circle us again.

They didn't wait for us to make another move. They attacked in a swarm, all at once; two, three, ten at a time, knocking Nox down and forcing her to drop us. I lost sight of Chelle and fell, crashing hard against the dome of the building. I sat, stunned, and considered my next move. If I could somehow disrupt the laser, it would delay the Spore's plans. My eyes went fuzzy as I balanced myself on the dome. Chelle was unconscious next to me, her body limp, pressed against a ledge to prevent her from sliding further.

As I climbed, straining against gravity and my body, the fight above me continued. Nox was holding her own against the gods, but she couldn't survive for long. Even if she was a powerful god, the Spore were eternal and infinite. Sound of battle filled the air: lightning crackling and thunder crashing, along with the explosions of a thousand hands. Finally, I reached the laser. It was a half dozen feet from me, a jump I could easily make but now, my legs could barely shuffle forward.

I pulled out a dagger and aimed it true. If I could catch one on the laser, maybe I could—maybe—but that's when my body gave up on me and I fell over the side of the laser into the dome below.

I couldn't save anybody; not anymore.

CHAPTER 43
ARIEL

A sinking feeling filled the pit of my stomach as I followed Vivian up the stairs of the dungeon. The green emerald made her skin glitter, and her smile still had the same poison in it when she looked back at me.

"Don't look so glum, sister," she said, tapping her feet on the ground like she was a ballerina, gleefully performing a recital. "It can't be so bad to spend time with me."

"I'm just waiting for the betrayal, Vivian," I replied, eyeing her coldly.

"Come now. When have I ever given you reason to distrust me?"

I laughed. "I know that's a joke, but it is in bad taste. It would be easier to tell you of the times you proved trustworthy, because I cannot think of one. Every moment I thought you might have changed, it was just deception that led to an even bigger betrayal."

"And what would I have to gain by betraying you this time, sister? They would surely find me before I left the castle, and there is a war going on, after all."

I almost asked how she knew, but the battle was raging

so loudly I could hear it. My blood turned to ice as I realized that the sound was much too loud to come from outside the castle, and when we moved through an intersection in the corridor, I saw the Emerald knights battling against horrors from the Nightmare Realm.

"Oh my," Vivian said. "We must hurry. There isn't much time."

She didn't move any faster, though. If anything, she seemed to skip down the hallway at the thought of the whole of the Dream Realm being overrun with monsters. A thought dawned on me—Vivian moved through the hallways as if she had been through them before, but she had always told me that the surface world was a hideous place she had no interest in visiting.

"Have you been here before?" I asked.

"What makes you say that?" Her words were snide but playful and it was infuriating in the way only a sibling could.

"Did Nox bring you here?"

Vivian spun on her heels. "Nox promised me rule of the Dream Realm often, even if they were hollow words. She told me that she would give me the land of Oz and all of Urgu if I swore that I loved her above all others."

"And did you?"

"Several times. But every time I asked about my rule, she told me it wasn't time yet. When she disappointed me, she brought me here, into her private chambers, as a way to satiate my desire."

We turned a corner and headed down a dark corridor. I questioned her further. "I thought you said that Nox's grotto was your special place. Or was that a lie?"

She hopped along beside me and smiled. "Everything I

ever say is a lie, my sister. I thought you would know that by now."

"Even the things that contradict each other?" I asked.

"Especially those things."

She wouldn't give me a real answer, but from her demeanor, I sensed that I knew the truth. "Loki told you where the sword was, didn't he? And how to get it?"

"Maybe," she said. "But I like my story better."

"So what? You get the sword, save the realm, and take the crown from Queen Aine at the same time?"

"So distrustful." She smiled as she came to a stop. "We're here."

The door was black and covered in hideous monsters that moved up the door like a waterfall in reverse, churning the most horrible water imaginable. She pushed on the door, and it groaned at her touch before it gave.

"Oh, good." She took a deep breath. "I wasn't sure that was going to work."

I followed her inside. The monsters of the Nightmare Realm drew closer, and it wouldn't be long before they overtook the whole of Urgu, if they hadn't already.

Nox's office was filled floor to ceiling with books, thousands of them on every surface, and a large leather-backed chair. A small table next to it held a small tea mug, filled with something left undrunk. Vivian reached forward and brought her finger to the mug. In a second it was gone, ingested into her skin, making it glow brighter.

"Pity," Vivian said. "She had such great plans for this realm. If only she hadn't been captured. Though, I suppose she must have escaped if—well, I suppose I'll ask her for a detailed summary if any of us survive this." She walked over to a bookshelf and muttered an incantation. With it, she reached into the air itself until she was elbow deep.

"This was all for show. She kept all the good stuff in the ether."

When her hand emerged, she held a sword. She twisted until I could see the hilt, and sure enough, there was an inscription. I didn't read elvish, and yet, I innately knew it read as "Hope Bringer."

"That's it!" I shouted, rushing forward.

She held it in the air, examining it. "This sword will make its wielder the new god of the Dream Realm—or goddess, as the case may be. Thank you for confirming its existence for me."

"So this is when you betray me?" I asked.

"Rude," she replied in a huff. "But yes, someth—"

I didn't wait for her to finish before I collapsed a bookcase down upon her. Then another, and finally a third. Vivian was formidable, but she loved herself too much to ever shut up. I reached down to her unconscious body and grabbed the sword.

It vibrated in my hand. *The new god of the Dream Realm, huh?* I hated the sound of that, but with the sounds of the monsters growing louder by the minute, there wasn't any other option left.

Enough equivocating, Ariel. Who was I, my sister? No. I was no longer a woman who waited. I was now a woman of action.

So, act.

CHAPTER 44

NIMUE

"I have placed the last glyph," Lydia bellowed into my head. "How are you doing?"

How was I doing? I had spent the last hours drawing sigils and glyphs in the abandoned buildings all over the Celestial Realm. We tested a modified version of Baba's circle on a smaller rock formation, and it worked without a hitch, so I sent the other princesses off to complete their tasks while I finished mine. We started on the outskirts of the realm and worked our way in until we were mere miles from the domed Oracle building where I surrendered Gabrielle to Nox.

The gods had not come for me, which told me that the Spore were not wise to my deception. "I'm nearly finished. Delilah?"

"I've just completed the last glyph, too," she replied. "And connected us telepathically."

"And so have I," Cassandra said in our heads. "Let us end this."

"Then meet at the tower and prepare for the final battle."

I stepped out of the empty building where I hid the glyph and looked out at the empty street. I intended to commit several acts of wanton destruction in the realm to solidify my words to the Spore, but there was nothing so pathetic as carnage without witnesses. I expected to see at least a few stragglers on the road, cowering in buildings or avoiding the Spore, but I didn't feel any heartbeats or hear any breathing as I made my way from building to building. Even the gods and goddesses controlled by the Spore had long since made their way to the domed building, drawn like moths to a flame.

The final step was connecting the glyphs at the base of Nox's tower so that when we initiated the chain reaction, it would splinter across the whole of the Celestial Realm and take it all down with a single snap of my fingers.

"You have betrayed us," several voices shouted as a trio of gods landed on either side of me. I had not understood how they could appear without breathing air or having a heartbeat. Even gods had blood. Then I realized that the dead eyes and decomposing skin meant they were reanimated monsters long since dead. I didn't know the Spore had that power and frankly, it frightened me. However, soon they would not be an issue anymore.

The gods they inhabited had been powerful and formidable enough on their own, let alone when they attacked as a swarm. I raised my hand and called forth a lightning storm that shot through each of my attackers for a full ten seconds. When the lightning stopped, their charred flesh sizzled, but they remained upright.

They advanced, and it was then I heard the battle cry of a dozen tiny voices in the night. I turned to see a cadre of monsters, elves, dwarves, humans, and other creatures running through the streets, shooting water pistols at the gods.

At first, I laughed at the pure foolishness of it, but then something amazing happened. The gods, after they swallowed a taste of the water, would shudder and fall to the ground. When they did, a mass of spores shot from their bodies. Before the spores could flee, the tiny hands of their attackers pulled out little boxes and muttered a spell. The boxes glowed brightly, and the Spore vanished in a flash of light.

"What just happened?" I asked.

A goat-horned man turned to me. "We just saved your life. Those gods would have killed you."

"I appreciate that, but what did you just do with those spores in the air?"

The boy shrugged. "I don't know. Zapped them into another plane of being, I guess."

"Come on, Flirzol," a reptilian girl called out to him. "We have a long way to go and a short time to get there."

"Right!" He turned back to me. "Good luck, citizen. Stay safe."

Before I could respond, the little one tipped his head to me and ran off. I would have sworn it was a group of clueless children if I didn't know otherwise. The troop of water soldiers zipped past me until only a small trickle of them remained, and in them, I saw a familiar face.

"Nimue?" Rose said, clutching a golden dagger tightly in her hand. "Of course, you would be here, at the end of the universe. You look terrible."

How did she recognize me after my transition into the King in Yellow's princess? Was I still so obvious, even after such a change?

"It's not what you think," I replied. "I'm trying—"

"I don't care what you are trying." She gritted her teeth. "We have unfinished business. The Spore can wait. You die now."

CHELLE

I appreciated that we went down fighting, but we still went down. I woke to the Spore tying a leather strap tight around my head. They wouldn't make the same mistake of using metal bracers again, clearly. The dome was filled with hundreds of the possessed gods, inspecting us to make sure that we could not move.

Red, lying next to me, looked just awful. The whole right side of her body was charred black, and what little of her face I could see had swelled with welts and bruises. Our bodies healed quickly. That hers still showed marks all over it meant she was grievously wounded and must have been in incredible pain.

Athena's voice boomed through the domed building as her body floated down toward us. "You made a valiant effort, but now you know that there is no stopping the inevitable."

"We will never stop fighting," Red groaned.

"I know that now," Athena replied. I hoped that Kadlu had killed her in our last battle, but the goddess must have simply been incapacitated. It was nearly impossible to kill a god, which made them perfect vessels for the Spore's plan. "And have made arrangements to make sure that you cannot, even given your best efforts."

"Please. You don't have to do this." Nox's voice was just as labored from the other side of me. She was strapped down even more forcefully than I was. I felt Hypnos's finger twitch above me and realized that my finger had been tied down so that I was forced into contact with him.

"I wouldn't have to do this if you simply understood the order of things and lived within them," Athena said. "But instead, you decided to take it upon yourselves to fight against us. You forced my brothers and sisters into oblivion, and all I am doing, all I have ever done, is try to bring them back and fix the mistake of your folly."

I'd had enough of her insanity. "You are going to punish the whole of the universe because you're pissed at the gods? Guess what? We're *all* pissed, but we don't have a temper tantrum and destroy everything because of it."

Athena chuckled. "You humans have the petulance and delusions of grandeur of your creators. You think I am punishing the universe just because you will be worse off. However, you do not think about how so many of our most beautiful creations have been punished for eons because the gods chose you as their favorites instead of the insects, arachnids, and creatures of the darkness which we favored."

"Gross," Red said with disdain.

"You only think that because you carry your maker's sense of disgust, but that which you disdain so well are your superiors. Do you not wonder why they seem to survive in conditions that would fell even the strongest of you? Do you not think that it is odd you are only able to survive on a few planets in the universe, and only in perfect conditions, while others seem to populate everywhere and everything? They are your betters. They are the true masters of the universe, and we only aim to right the balance which the gods upended."

"We took up arms because you were cruel and inhumane," Nox said, trying her best to speak through gritted teeth.

"To you!" Athena boomed. "You never understood us. No matter. It will all be over soon."

The world fell away as a piercing noise filled the air. The pain started numbly, and then began to fill every muscle in my body, from the tips of my fingers and toes, up through my shins and forearms, until it crept into my shoulders and thighs.

By the time it filled my chest, the pain was unbearable, and then, in a sudden burst, it shot from me, and I felt my soul pulled from my body into the sky above. A red beam of pure energy and power fired from the base of the dome and shot a hundred feet into the air into a second, piercing the sky, which filled with a brilliant light.

It would all be over soon.

CHAPTER 46

ROSE

She was there, right in front of me. The horrible witch responsible for everything bad in my life. She tried to kill me in the Dream Realm. She fought to destroy the Fairy Realm, and now Nimue stood, looking directly at me, wearing a stupid smile. It didn't matter that her skin was cracked with black ichor, like her body had been pulled apart by the darkest depths of the universe. I would recognize her face anywhere.

"You bitch!" I tossed a scorching ray of fire in her direction.

"Stop!" Nimue growled, deflecting the spell with one hand. "I am not your enemy!"

"You will always be my enemy!" I called forth a dozen ice spikes and shot them at her.

"What is with you children holding grudges?" Again, Nimue dispelled my magic, sending water falling to the ground. "If you are trying to destroy the Spore, then we are on the same team this time!"

"I don't believe you!"

"I don't care!" Nimue shouted back. "I am not the same

person that you fought all those moons ago. I have changed into something new."

I called forth an arc of lightning from the sky and sent it shooting down upon her. "You can change your skin, but you will always be the same evil in your heart."

Nimue caught the lightning in her arms and redirected it into a nearby building, sending one of its walls crashing to the ground. "Have you not noticed I haven't retaliated to your petulance, even though I could destroy you with a thought?"

"Perhaps you are weaker than you let on," I replied, snarling. I was chomping at the bit for a fight. "If you are not sending your full force against me, then there must be a reason."

Nimue sighed, and without another word sent down a hailstorm of fireballs onto me and shot an arc of lightning from her wrist. I tried to stop the attack, but her attack was more powerful than I imagined it could be. I took down two fireballs, but a half dozen more reached me. The force of their explosions against the shield I'd thrown up rocked me backwards and sent me tumbling across the ground.

I knocked against the side of a building as I stopped, whacking my head into the brick. I watched the bolt of lightning arc toward me, but I was too spent to even hold up a shield, or duck to the side.

I closed my eyes and tensed, preparing for the impact, but it never came. I opened my eyes and saw the lightning holding steady an inch from my heart. I locked eyes with Nimue, who nodded slightly before the bolt dissipated into the air.

"Please know, child, that I am more powerful than you can fathom. I have used every trick at my disposal to build myself into this visage, and every ounce of my wit to exploit its power. I choose not to hurt you, and that is the only reason you live right now. If I willed it, then you would die at my hand this instant."

"This doesn't change anything, witch," I said, rising to my feet.

"You'll have to change your mind if you want to save your girlfriend."

That stopped me. "What do you know about Chelle?"

"I know that she is being held by the Spore—" As Nimue spoke, an enormous red bolt of energy, brighter than a star, illuminated the sky and shot high into space. It was as if morning came to the Celestial Realm, as the light cascaded over everything. "She's in incredible danger right now. If we don't save her, the entire universe is in danger."

"Why do you care? The Spore seem like your kind of people."

"You have known me as well as any," she growled. "Do you think I have any desire to be ruled by tyrants?"

I pursed my lips. "No, I can say that for sure."

"Well, the Spore intend to rule the universe with their brethren, and they will not look kindly to my kind or yours."

"So you would save the gods, then?" I asked, walking toward her. "You would cure them of their Spore infestation?"

"I don't much care to save them or cure them. The gods are vain and feckless. They have no clue how to rule a universe, and because of that, their tyranny is comical at best...but I hate the Spore even more and would see them all burn today. If I save the gods in the process, that is fine, I suppose. If I char them to cinder, all the better." Nimue must have seen my face contort in horror, because her voice softened along with her face. "For my part, I can promise you that I have no intention of destroying you, or the universe. I have only ever aimed to live free. I have made mistakes, to be sure, but I would rather die than live under the tyranny of the gods or the Primordials. It is time to let humanity guide itself, as much as it can."

"I hate you, you know?" I said.

"And I don't think about you at all, but you are powerful enough to be an asset." She looked up into the sky as three figures came down on us. I held up my arms to attack, but she held up her hands. "They are with me."

"Who is this?" one of them asked. She had the silhouette of a forest growing all over her body.

"An old nemesis," Nimue replied, giving me a significant look. "Who I think has agreed to help us, yes?"

"We could use the help," a woman bathed in fire replied. "We clocked a hundred gods headed into this direction. I think that they know we have deceived them."

"Then it is time to end this," Nimue said. "We have to set one sigil at the bottom of the tower, and then we can end this. Tell me, will you help us?"

My eyes narrowed. "I do not trust you, but I have no choice but to help you if it will save Chelle."

"Rose," Nimue said. "It will save everything."

"Then I am with you."

I couldn't believe the words were coming out of my mouth, but one thing I knew was that Nimue would get whatever she wanted, by any means necessary, and if she aimed to destroy the Spore, then our goals were aligned, even if just only.

RED

My mind took me back to a time when I was just a child. It was my birthday, before Papa succumbed to consumption and before Mama needed money and one less mouth to feed—back when we were happy. I was given a book of poetry. My first book, a book that became my first obsession.

I didn't even remember reading for the last several hundred years, not since the days before the Dream Realm. That girl, the simple girl with her simple pleasures, was lost to me. My love of books was stolen from me by my husband. He was more my jailer than anything, and though slowly I grew to care for him, he never cared for me in the same way. I was only a thing to him, and in trying to please him, I lost every part of myself I ever loved.

It was a simple but difficult life, and I had to dream. I aimed to become more than my station, to become useful, to make sure nobody ever suffered again. If I had only stayed on that farm, with my nose buried in a book, maybe none of this would have happened, and I wouldn't be used to help destroy the universe.

The pain flooded back to me in wave after wave until I couldn't think of anything else—until I was pulled back to the domed building, the maniacal Spore, and the end of my life.

My hands turned to ash as they were sucked back into the universe. I was so focused on the future, and my vengeance, I never took the time to love, or to learn, or to read more—the simple pleasures were lost to me, and now I would never have a chance to lose myself in them again.

CHAPTER 48

ARIEL

"Sister!" Vivian screamed at me. "Get back here!"

I needed to get to the throne room. I pushed open the door to Nox's chamber and rushed up the corridor. I didn't think she would escape so quickly, but she slid out of the door behind me. She was hobbling and enfeebled, but she still moved forward. With any luck I could avoid her and make my way into the throne room without issues but—

Pain like I'd never felt gripped me, and I fell to the ground. I looked down at my hands and they had begun to disintegrate. Just the very tips of my fingers, but I could tell my soul was being wiped out, and it meant that the ritual had begun. I hoped that somebody would save me and destroy the machine, but it wasn't to be.

All I had to do was get to the throne room before death took me. Time moved differently in Urgu, slower than on the outside, so I hoped to have minutes instead of seconds to finish my quest and end my life with a purpose.

I used the hilt of the sword to pull myself up and steady my feet. Vivian moved slowly and had barely gained on my position in her pained state, which meant as long as I maintained my pace, I should be able to make it.

"Leave me alone!" I shouted back as I limped up the corridor. The slick surface didn't make it any easier, but I managed to turn down another hallway. Ash from my feet filled the air as the tips of my toes disappeared.

I stumbled forward to the intersection where the guards had fought monsters, only to see all the Emerald guards disintegrating or strewn on the floor, defeated. The same scene played out as I moved through the hallways, trying desperately to find my way to the throne room.

It wasn't long before my strength drained from me, and I had to stop to catch my breath. The pain burned through me, and it was hard to move forward, but I couldn't stop. I started back down the hall when something smashed into my back and sent me sliding across the floor.

Vivian snarled at me. "You will not take this from me!" She crashed between the gemmed walls as she went for the sword.

I lunged for her and pulled her to the ground. Neither of us had the strength to kill the other. It was a battle of wills, and I would not fall to hers ever again. She kicked at me, but my eyes flashed pink, and I pushed her away.

My powers. I still had my powers. I had forgotten them in the fracas, but if I could get to the sword maybe I could teleport to the throne room. My body was turning to ash, and I had little more hope than to get to the room before I passed away for good.

"Enough!" I slammed my hands into her, and she vaporized in an instant.

I had killed my sister. I took no joy in it, but there was no time for being delicate.

I used what was left of my hands to pull myself to the

sword, and with another flash of pink, I thought of the throne room and vanished. I reappeared in a darkened room, filled with every type of creature cowering. The doors cracked from each side of the hallway. Monsters and horrible beings growled from the other side and smashed against the doors until they were torn from the hinges.

"Ariel!" I looked up to see Queen Aine floating toward me. "My gods, it's good to see you."

I tried to stand, but my feet gave out under me. "No time—help me to the throne."

"I don't—" She must have seen the pink flame in my eyes, because she snapped her fingers and two dirty, bruised guards stood through the rabble and made their way over to her. "Bring her to the throne."

They carried me to the throne and propped me against it.

"We're here," Aine said. "Now what?"

"Have them push the throne forward." My words were weak, and it felt like my whole body was on fire. "Quickly."

Queen Aine nodded, and the soldiers did as I asked. The throne didn't move easily, but after the longest, most torturous minutes of my life, they were able to slide it forward enough to reveal a hole in the ground, just big enough to slide a sword through.

"What is that?" Queen Aine asked.

I crawled forward on my elbows, and with the last of my strength gathered to my knees. "Salvation."

I raised the sword into the air and slid it into place. I thought only of Urgu as my body split apart into a thou-sand, million pieces. Every bit of me exploded throughout the Dream Realm, pushing the monsters back through the holes from whence they came. They broke apart into dust until the Dream Realm was free.

The only one I saved was Canterbury. A small piece of my soul fell on him and protected him from my magic, allowing him to remain in Urgu for his service to me.

And with that, I floated off into eternity, a god for only a moment, but doing as much as any in my short time with infinity.

CHAPTER 49
NIMUE

The horde of gods came at us the moment we hit the air. They fired on us, and the sky erupted into mountains of destruction.

"Stick by me!" Rose said.

I didn't have a better option, so I followed her down to the ground, where the resistance was fighting their own horde of gods and goddesses. Rose grabbed one of the water guns from one of their fallen bodies and flew back up into the air.

"What are you doing?" I asked.

"Spray it into their mouths!"

I was confused until I watched her do it. The god fell to the ground and crashed next to me, unmoving. When I looked at it more closely, there was no longer any black ichor in its eyes.

The god stirred, blinking. "What—happened?"

I took a water gun from one of the other dead children and shoved it into the god's hands. "We saved you, and if you value your life, I suggest you grab a gun and join us."

"You have to be kidding me," Lydia said into my brain. "That is the dumbest—"

I kicked off the ground and flew into the air. "If we can turn these gods back, then maybe we can turn the tide."

"And what if they learn we're trying to destroy their world?" Delilah's voice joined Lydia's. It was the easiest way to communicate during battle.

"Just don't tell them, and in the very unlikely scenario that they figure it out before we destroy them, we'll take it from there. I would much rather deal with those gods then the Spore, wouldn't you?"

"Touché," Cassandra chimed in, ducking down to get her own gun with Delilah and Lydia.

I fired multiple lightning strikes at the gods to redirect them, and when they were off balance, I shot my water gun into two of their mouths. Much to my delight, their eyes also turned from black to dark blue.

"If you wish to save your brethren, then I suggest you join us!" I shouted.

Soon we had a little army fighting back against the Spore, with a dozen gods on our side and more turning every second. When we had enough to make a push forward, I pulled Rose back.

"We need to make a final assault," I shouted. I hadn't let her in the chain of voices in my head with the princesses. "They're just toying with us until the ritual is done."

"Agreed. I think with our powers combined we can create a path."

"At least to buy us a little time, but they will collapse it right when we are through."

She sighed. "I always thought this would be a one-way trip, and I'm willing to make that sacrifice if we should fail."

I wasn't, but I didn't tell her that. "Good, then on my count."

I pulled back to where Lydia, Cassandra, and Delilah were working on their own cohort of gods. I ushered them over to the other gods who were on our side.

"Alright!" I shouted. "Everyone use as much power as you can muster to push us through this horde RIGHT NOW!"

In one massive blast we brought all our power to bear, shooting several beams of power and creating a small gap through the endless gods blotting out everything. In their wake, I saw the domed building, and the red light shooting from the top of it.

The light above the laser had begun to shift as a little hole was cut into it. Monsters of unimaginable horror wriggled their tentacles through the barrier between our universes. In mere minutes, they would be through.

"ONE MORE TIME!" I shouted, and with this beam Rose and I rushed inside while the others joined us to hold back the onslaught.

The crazy monsters sprinted toward us as they realized our plan, shooting beams of fire, water, and earth at us with every movement we made. The beams nicked at my arms and legs, but I was able to avoid their blows, if just barely.

Lydia screamed. Gods surrounded her, firing lasers and other beams at her until she broke apart and fell to the ground. Our connection was severed, and Delilah looked at me in horror. She clearly didn't want this to be her last stand, but it didn't matter. The gods fell on her all the same, and the same fate came to her.

Cassandra was next. She looked at me one last time and closed her eyes. The heap of gods began to vibrate, and then an incredible explosion of light filled the air. Cassandra was nowhere to be seen, but the gods surrounding her were knocked backward. It gave me an idea.

"*Sunburst!*" I shouted and pulled Rose toward me. An immense explosion sent several gods tumbling away and opened a clear path to the base of the building. It was not as powerful as Cassandra's final spell, but it did the trick all the same.

"We can't hold them off for long!" Rose shouted as we neared the building.

"We need a new army."

Rose and I sprayed our water guns into as many mouths as we could until neither of us had a drop left. Together we saved twenty or so gods. They were loyal enough for our purposes. Maybe they would even be saved for their service, but I doubted it.

"If you value your freedom, create a barrier!" I shouted. "We need five minutes, and if they get through your whole universe is doomed."

Their realm was doomed already, but the whole universe would be damned if they couldn't hold off their brethren.

"Go save your girl," I said to Rose. "In a couple minutes, she won't have the chance to escape."

Rose nodded and pushed off into the air. She might have thought it was a magnanimous gesture, but really I just needed somebody to distract the Spore while I worked away. They couldn't direct all their attacks at me if Rose was going in to save her girlfriend. They might not even see me as a threat, even though I was their biggest one.

I watched Rose rise into the sky and I began to build my glyph, which would link them all together and destroy everything. I only wished that Lydia, Cassandra, and Delilah had survived long enough to enjoy it with me.

CHAPTER 50
CHELLE

Hold it together, Chelle. Hold it TOGETHER!

My gods. The pain.

The pain.

My soul was being ripped from my body inch by bloody inch, and the power from it was being sucked up into the—

It was too painful to thi—

Think about.

But I would not die. I would fight. I would fight. I would *fight!*

CHAPTER 51
"ROSE"

All my thoughts turned to Chelle when I landed on the platform outside of the Spore's domed base that they called the Oracle. I held my golden dagger ready as the Spore began to attack en masse. There were few things that could kill a god, but the golden dagger Red bequeathed me could slice through them with one cut, sending them to the great beyond.

It might not have been their fault that the Spore controlled their bodies, but the gods had done enough across their existence that I didn't feel too bad carving through them. Perhaps some of them were good, but not good enough. The vast majority took their power for granted and expected everyone to kowtow to them.

"Chelle!" I said, slicing through one's stomach as I threw a fireball into a pair of other gods. Without the dagger, I would have been outmatched, but it put me on par with the Spore, and the more I fought, the more I realized they were quite basic as fighters.

The Spore lived for an eternity, but they had clearly spent very little of that time practicing fighting. They expected the sheer mass of their numbers would overwhelm anything that tried to attack them. They played on the fact that the gods were all-powerful to force their hands, but with precision strikes I could take them out easily. Their attacks were sloppy, and they swung with brute force that could be easily avoided with a little practice.

Charging through the base, I thought about those first days in the Dream Realm, when Red and Chelle had to guard me, to protect me, and to train me so I wouldn't die. I thought about how I was betrayed by the Church of the Five, and everything that had happened since. Never had I imagined that I would be powerful enough to stand up against a single god, let alone hundreds of them, and yet time hardened me, and love emboldened me.

I would not lose Chelle. The thought of it was unimaginable. If she died again, she would evaporate into nothingness, and nothing was more painful than that thought, not even the end of the universe.

Behind me, the dead gods I'd eviscerated rose from the dead, the Spore attacking with them, but I continued toward the center of the Oracle. Hopefully Nimue's plan would work, and when her explosion went off, the Spore would all fall down dead. Otherwise, I would be no savior today.

"*Industria murum!*" I shouted when I finally reached a door where the screams of my love, and my friend, were nearly deafening. My spell raised an energy wall that separated me from the horde of monstrous gods. They would break through soon, but I needed a moment to save my friends and escape.

I shot a fireball and the door bent but didn't break. I shot three more and finally got through. Inside, a hundred gods hovered above me. Red and Chelle laid on metal slabs, bathed in red, disintegrating. There were three other slabs, but they were empty except for dust rising from their spots, as if whatever laid there had been dusted, and nothing of them remained.

"*Industria murum!*" I shouted again, and an energy wall rose above me, covering the dome, and separated the gods from me. There were still a half dozen others managing the controls, and I fried them with fireballs.

"No!" the Spore shouted in unison.

I moved through them quickly, evading their blows easily, and redirecting their magic to fry the machines. Once I'd skewered the last one through the chest, I slashed the leather restraints on Chelle's bands, pulling her from the machine. She was weak and pale, but she looked at me with a smile.

"Don't move, okay?" I said.

"You came for me," she whispered.

"Always," I replied, kissing her cheek.

Red had been through the ringer and was hanging on by a thread, her body nearly transparent. I ripped her from the leather straps and could barely catch hold of her but managed to wrap her under one arm and Chelle in the other.

The gods had broken through my energy shield. Now it was all on Nimue. I kicked off the ground just as the earth quaked. A wave of sonic energy shot through me and into the air. The gods fell to the ground screaming, landing in the flames that followed the sound wave.

The path in front of me was clear, but the explosion rocked me from side to side and shook me to my core. I nearly lost hold of Red twice before I broke through the dome. I started out over the Celestial Realm, but there was another sonic wave, followed by a third. Together, they destabilized me, and I barreled toward the ground. I braced for impact and called forth a shield to protect us, but when I smashed into the rock below, I lost hold of Red and the golden dagger, and I slid with Chelle across the exploding ground.

CHAPTER 52
RED

I tried to place my hand on the ground when I opened my eyes, but my body could not find purchase. I grabbed futilely for something to steady myself, but my hands swiped through everything I tried to touch. I was fading out of existence and fading fast. Even though there was no longer the blistering pain of losing my soul, I knew the damage was irreversible.

"Chelle! Chelle!" Rose shouted. I turned to see her leaning over Chelle's lifeless body, nearly as broken as mine. "*Sana! Sana! Sana!*"

It would not work. No magic could help us now, but perhaps, if I could get there, I could stabilize her with what was left of my energy. I gathered my strength and once again tried to place my hand down. This time it worked, and I clawed my way over.

"Move," I rasped and managed to push Rose away. I placed my hands inside of Chelle and focused my energy. She was phasing through the ground, which rumbled around us. The Celestial Realm was breaking apart, and the molten goo that held it together bubbled like Tartarus. "Come on, Chelle! Come on!"

My body burned while my energy coursed through her. She blinked furiously in and out of existence, and then a great force jolted through her. It knocked me back to the ground and I felt cold steel against my hand when I landed. The golden dagger.

"Maybe I can help." The voice bristled the hairs on the back of my neck.

Nimue.

In one motion, I grabbed the dagger, whirled, and thrust it into Nimue's chest before she had a chance to betray us again. She stumbled backward, something like black ink oozing from her chest, and dropped to the ground with a thud. I had chased her around the universe, and now, finally, she got the justice she deserved. Then my chest tightened, and I sank to the ground. The dagger sank through my hands, and my arms were transparent.

"Red!" Rose screamed, sprinting to my side. She tried to place her hand on my back, but it ran right through me with a cold chill, and she stumbled. She sobbed. "No, you can't go."

"Did—" I took a deep breath. "Is Chelle—did I—?"

She nodded. "I don't know what you did, but she stopped fading. Look."

I turned my head and saw that it was true. Chelle was solid again, and I smiled at the thought of saving my friend. "Good, good. Then, at least I have done one good thing."

I spent my whole life trying to do good...trying to be good...and now, at the end, at least I managed to do it at least once. My eyes faded and all I could see was white, as Rose wailed. I wanted to protect her. I wanted to tell her it would be okay.

But there was nothing left inside of me, and I broke apart, returning to the universe.

CHAPTER 53
NIMUE

No, this could not be the end.

And yet, I knew it was. I watched Rose howl over Gabrielle as the Red Rider faded into nothingness, but there was nobody to cry for me. I had not affected anyone enough to weep over my body, and there were none left to sing my praises. I would be the evil witch in every story, in every realm, for eternity.

I pulled the dagger out, but it only made the black ichor rush out faster. "*Sana,*" I whispered, placing my hand on my chest, but nothing happened. I tried again, and again my body didn't heal. She must have cut me with a blade meant to fell a god. There was nothing I could do to stop the bleeding once it punctured my cold, black heart. There was nothing to do but embrace the cold sting of death.

I brought it on myself, I supposed. Strong, confident women were always seen as the bad one, the squeaky wheels, and the witches. I was not proud of all I had done in my life, but I lived for an eternity, and had seen more of the universe than most.

And I saved people. I defeated Etsop. I ended the reign

of the Winter Court. I stopped the King in Yellow. I was out for myself, perhaps, but I did good in the process. No matter what anyone else said, I did good in the world.

All I ever wanted was to live free.

I sank to my knees. I doubted I would end up in the Dream Realm, or the Underworld. Those were not places for monsters like me. I would bleed back into the universe, like the gods who made me.

"Nimue!" Rose shouted when her wet eyes connected with mine. She rushed over to me. "I'm so sorry. You were right. You were trying to save us. I didn't think—"

"It's okay," I replied, pointing to the book that held Elvira's soul. At least she could survive. "Take...the book, please..."

"I don't understand," she said.

"Please..." My voice was faint. "If you felt nothing else for me, do this one thing."

"Okay," she said. "I will."

I chuckled, black ichor falling from my hands. "Maybe I wasn't so bad, in the end."

Hundreds of gods landed around us. Their eyes were no longer black. Rose watched them and said, "I suppose not. I think you saved us all, even though you destroyed everything in the process."

"That sounds like me."

Just think, when I thought only of myself, I lived; it was only in thinking of the universe for once, that I finally succumbed to the sweet release of death.

Maybe it wouldn't be so bad to stop existing. There were no thrones for people like me. There was no Valhalla. There was only punishment, and pain. Given that...I would prefer nothingness, and that's where I would return.

CHAPTER 54

CHELLE

I fell into darkness, and then with a jerk I returned to the world of the living. Rose was kneeling next to a body in a pool of black ichor. "Rose?"

Rose whipped around and cried out, "Chelle! You're alive!" She picked up the golden dagger at her side and a thick book and scrambled over to me.

"I don't know if that's true, but I think that I'm not dying at least." The ground rumbled. "I definitely think this whole place is falling apart, though."

Rose nodded, her tears a mixture of pain and happiness. "We need to go, now."

"And Red?" I asked. Rose's head fell to her chest, and she sobbed. "I'm so sorry."

Rose sniffled, then wrapped my arm around her shoulder and picked me up. "We can grieve later. Now, we have to go." She placed the book and dagger into my hands. "Hold these."

She pulled me into the air through the raining bodies of gods and goddesses. We weaved between them, the Celestial Realm breaking into pieces, as if a giant earthquake had ripped through the whole of the world and cracked it apart.

Molten lava spat up out of the fissures and swallowed the earth. We swerved left, and then right, and then picked up speed. We scanned the ground as we went, looking for any survivors, but there looked to be very few, if any, who survived the attack.

Rose landed on the edge of a water tower and dropped inside. "Wait for me!"

She must have been crazy to think I wouldn't go with her. I eased myself down and asked, "Where are we going?"

"I thought I said—" Rose said, a hint of exasperation in her voice. "Never mind. Look for Maricel. Maricel!"

I scanned the water until I saw a body bobbing up and down in the water supply. "There!"

Rose dove into the water, and I followed behind, kicking fast until we reached the body at the same time. She turned Maricel over and felt her chest. "She's alive, but only barely."

We pulled her to the side together and performed CPR on her, Rose pumping her chest and me breathing into her mouth. Eventually, Maricel turned to her side and coughed up water.

"Thank you," she croaked when she had finished coughing. The tower swerved back and forth, and the metal groaned.

"Thank me later," Rose said. "Can you fly?"

Maricel nodded. "I think so."

Rose wrapped her arms around me, and we kicked off the ground, shooting out of the water tower before it was swallowed into the molten rock.

"Follow me!" Maricel said, shooting through the city.

I held tightly to Rose's shoulder as she darted between

the buildings. They twisted and turned over as they toppled into the molten rock below. I didn't know where we were headed until I saw the terminal floating in the sea of molten lava.

The roof had been ripped clean off and laid in pieces. We'd just landed and Maricel was already rushing to the controls. She punched in numbers and turned dials.

"The portals are losing stability. I think I can get you back to your planet. Give me your hand!"

Rose placed her hand on the platform, and Maricel pricked her finger. With her blood on the console, one of the terminals flickered to life. "Is that it?"

"I don't know!" Maricel had to shout to be heard over the sounds of the terminal falling apart around us. "But it's the best I can do right now. We have to go!"

She pushed the two of us into the portal and followed behind us. The light flickered until it went dark, and we tumbled through into the world once again. I looked up to see the cool skies of the Swiss Alps above me.

It smelled like home, and so did Rose.

CHAPTER 55

ROSE

"Cheyenne! We're home!" I shouted as we entered the apartment that we left what felt like decades ago.

A tiny white fluffball scampered from around the corner and scrambled toward us. She jumped into my arms and licked my face for a full minute before sending out a huge, happy aroo that thundered through the room.

Chelle knelt and petted her when I set her down. Jamil, who'd been watching our interaction but giving us space, walked over. She took me into her arms for a big hug, and then did the same for Chelle.

"Hell of a vacation," she said.

Chelle laughed. "That was anything but a vacation."

"No," Jamil replied with a grin, "I meant a vacation for me. I started to think you weren't coming back and I was gonna be able to squat here forever."

"Well, soon enough the bills would come."

"You have more money than the gods, though, so it wouldn't affect me much." She stretched. "I guess it's time to get back to my old life."

"Yes," I replied. "And for us too, which will be a nice change of pace."

"I'll bet. Well, the fridge is stocked." She handed me my credit card. "I went bananas with it, so don't faint when you see the bill. After the second week, I figured that I was owed something nice for my service."

"Oh, most definitely," Chelle said. "Whatever we paid you, it's not enough."

"Wait until you see the bill to say that. I'm very expensive."

Jamil wasn't lying. She had weekly pedicures and nightly feasts that would make a king blush, but it was all worth it, because Cheyenne seemed happy, fat, and well-groomed. I decided not to tell Jamil about the gods—not yet at least. Not until I knew the extent of the destruction.

In my dreams, I visited Urgu and heard tales of the destruction Nox and the Nightmare Realm had wrought. A single girl saved them all before sacrificing herself for the good of the realm. She sent out her energy far and wide, closing up hundreds of holes ripped between their realms, giving them a chance to rebuild.

Chelle told me that the girl must have been Ariel, another one of the sacrifices that the Spore planned to use to destroy the universe. Nox and Hypnos never returned, and we assumed they were also sacrificed to open the barrier between our universe and the Primordials. I was the most powerful being in Urgu, since I still carried Hypnos's blessing, even with his untimely demise, so I helped them rebuild what they lost as best that I could.

We left the sword locked in the stone under the throne. We couldn't have moved it if we tried. Instead of being forced into Hypnos's vision of the world, Queen Aine and the others had a say in the reconstruction of Urgu, and what they couldn't do with magic, they built with their own two hands.

With the Dream Realm on its way to thriving again, I decided to take a trip to the Underworld and speak with Persephone. The Underworld was insulated from the destruction of the Celestial Realm. I brought Chelle through Limbo and into the palace throne room, where Persephone sat in front of the wall of fire by herself. Hades's throne had been removed.

"I didn't expect to see you again so soon," she said with a sly smile. "Have you died already?"

"No, ma'am. We thought you should know that the Celestial Realm has been destroyed. We hoped you had information we could use to find the extent of the damage."

The news was shocking to Persephone. While she went about finding more information, Chelle and I stayed in the opulent palace. The Obsidian Spindle no longer worked, but she had her own means of contacting the gods, or what remained of them after the final battle with the Spore.

"I have somber news," she told me after three days locked in her chambers. "What you have said is true, and the gods have been splintered around the galaxy, locked off from each other. The Obsidian Spindles connected us for generations, but now we are on our own."

"And the Spore?" I asked.

"Based upon what you told us, we are relatively certain that the Spore have been destroyed completely, but they are very tricky. If even one survives, they can come back. We must be ever vigilant."

"And what about the tear in the universe?"

Persephone sighed. "It seems too small for anything to get through right now, but it is ripping further. We have no way to seal it right now, but we hope it will take thousands of years for the Primordials to be able to break through, and we will hopefully have a solution before then."

I scoffed. "What if you don't?"

"Let us not think like that now. Let us look at the positive. You have saved the universe, both of you, yet again. We are, all of us, in your debt."

"We'll remember that," Chelle said with a smile, which turned down quickly. "So what about my condition?"

She shrugged. "We know very little about Primordial magic, and the one who knew the most has vanished from existence. Please have people in the Dream Realm look through her things, and if you find anything, bring it back here."

"I will. Meanwhile, I think it's time we head back. The Underworld does horrible things with my complexion."

"I have a cream for that."

"She was being polite," Chelle replied. "We want to go home."

"Fair enough. If any in the universe have earned it, then you have."

CHAPTER 56

CHELLE

"Have you seen my black dress?" Rose called from the bathroom.

We had moved from New York City to a small farm in Montana several months ago but, despite both of us having powerful magic, we had most of our stuff in boxes.

"Which one?" I had been ready for nearly an hour. Then again, I was wearing the same black pants and shirt that I usually did, except I'd added a jacket and a red ascot for the occasion.

"The long one. It's a somber occasion, so I figured I should wear the long dress."

"You realize you could just create it when we get there. You literally are the most powerful person in Urgu."

"That's cheating!" I shouted. "Red wouldn't want me to cheat."

I stood up from the Steelers game and walked into the bedroom. She had half the bedroom boxes on the floor and was sorting through them. I turned to the closet and opened a single box. I pulled out the dress and ran my hand over it to brush out all the wrinkles.

"Here you go," I said with a smile.

She snatched it from me and planted a kiss on my lips. "Thank you. I'll be ready in five."

I walked down the stairs and out the front door. The wheat fields whipped in the wind, and Cheyenne barked at our chickens. She liked it nearly as much as me. Rose didn't seem to have settled yet, but the silence did wonders for my constitution. Besides, she spent most of her days in the Dream Realm and disappeared whenever the world unmoored her.

She had power here, but in the Dream Realm, it was almost absolute. She was important there, and she still liked to feel important. I wanted what was best for her, so I supported her restlessness as long as she came home at the end of the day.

I hadn't been back to the Dream Realm for a long time, but Rose had planned something special to memorialize Red, and I agreed to go, even though the thought of it sent shivers down my spine.

"Ready," Rose said a few minutes later. I wasn't sure how many because I got lost in the fields, which was where my mind went most days.

She grabbed my hand and pulled me around to the barn. She had created a door to the Dream Realm in the back, with two-way access only to her. Nox and Hypnos would not have approved, but they were vaporized, leaving us in charge.

Most of the gods had died in the great Spore war, which left a power vacuum in the universe. Some said they would return to rebuild the Celestial Realm, but nobody seemed particularly interested in getting too close to the tear in the universe that I'd helped create.

We walked into Nox's study, which was directly on the

other side of the door. Rose spent a lot of time trying to determine what Nox knew about the universe, but it had been fruitless as of yet. Still, she was determined to figure it out, if there was anything to figure out.

We made our way up to the throne room where we met Queen Aine coming out with her entourage. She wore a black dress and veil. Her purple body glowed more dimly than usual, and she spoke with a whisper.

"It's good to see you."

Rose nodded. "You too."

"I'm sorry it always happens to be in these circumstances."

"Me too," I said. "But at least the world isn't falling apart right now."

Queen Aine sighed. "I suppose that is something."

The procession led us outside to the sculpture garden, and through the various heroes of the Dream Realm. A small group had gathered, all dressed in black, around a new statue, that of a woman in a red hood, holding daggers in each hand, ready to leap into battle.

We stood in the back as Balor, Red's oldest friend, climbed the step to a small stage. "Red was my best friend. I loved her more than that, even, but I never spoke the words to her out loud, so I don't know if she felt the same way. I regret that. I'm sorry she is gone. There is a giant hole in the universe nothing will ever fill. However, she died as she lived: valiantly and bravely fighting for what is true and seeking justice for us all. She died getting vengeance on the Wicked Witch Nimue, who terrorized us for so long. With her dying breath, Red thought only of valor and honor." He cleared his throat. "I wish to thank Rose, who constructed this statue and poured into it the love she had for her friend. Rose, if you would, please, come up and say a few words."

Rose walked forward and hugged Balor, tears already falling down her face. She composed herself and began to speak. "Red was the best friend I ever knew and the most loyal person I ever met. I miss her every day, and I hope her memory lives on in this statue, and in the hearts of us all. She seemed immortal to me, too strong to ever die, and yet, death comes for us all, in time. Hold close those you care for and cherish them. Even in this place, cherish what you have, because it can all be taken away in an instant. We of Urgu know that more than most, but I still take it for granted more often than I care to admit. Red taught me how to be brave in the face of injustice, and she taught me how to love recklessness, even when everything was on the line. I have lost everything more times than I can count, but so had Red, and she still chose to force the arc of history to bend toward justice. I will never forget her, and I hope you will not either, because everyone deserves a friend like Red."

Rose walked back toward me. She held it together during her speech, but she fell apart into my arms, sobbing uncontrollably as guards fired muskets into the air. When they were done, Queen Aine took the stage.

"Before we depart, I would be remiss if we did not name another hero. Ariel of the Forgotten Sea, blessed by Hypnos, and god of dreams. She saved us from the horrors of the Nightmare Realm, and so I would like to direct your attend to the side of the Emerald Castle."

Aine pointed to the side of the building, where an enormous statue of a woman floated into the air, hands outstretched, looking down on all Urgu. As we watched, the statue rose higher and higher until it was taller than the castle, where it stopped and hovered over everything.

"We will use our fairy magic to keep it afloat every day until the end of time, as a reminder of the weight she carried, and what we carry now in her honor. Gods bless you, Ariel, as we do."

With that, the group disbanded, and we said our goodbyes. We walked through the streets, and I marveled at what Rose had built from nothing once again.

"I'm tired," she eventually said, leaning against my shoulder, and we walked back to the door that led us back to our home. Cheyenne rushed to meet us when we were in the Montana grass again, and together the three of us walked into the house.

The future was uncertain, but for now, we were happy enough with a simple life, the kind of life we wanted all along, and what more could you ask for?

AUTHOR'S NOTE

The end of book twelve is here, and that wraps up the third arc of The Obsidian Spindle Saga. The first three books had only one point of view character dying, which isn't normal for me, but this last book made up for it since we killed three main characters, including two that have been point of view characters since the first book. It was painful for me to see Red and Nimue go, but it was the right time.

Before I get to those two, I need to talk about Ariel. I planted the seed for her back in book 4, and I thought she would be a POV character in the second arc. In fact, book 6 was originally called *The Drowned Princess*, which ended up being the name for book 10. It was a really long seed, but I think it paid off in this arc. Originally, when I wrote this outline, Ariel was due to be tortured for most of the book, but that didn't seem fair to a POV character that had been a main character in three other books.

I thought maybe it would make sense to show that death is capricious and sometimes there is not some big destiny for you, but that seemed antithetical to the point of this book series, which is that good people can rise up and take control of their destiny. So, I felt really good about having her save the Dream Realm and becoming a god, if only for a moment. It was a bear to make sure that her journey lined up with the rest of the plot, especially since it wasn't part of the original outline, but I hope she had a satisfying arc. She started with a tiny role and ended up as a hugely important character. I really loved her as a character, even if she only carried the story for a short time.

Okay, now on to the two deaths that rocked me the most.

First, Red.

Red was one of the first characters that I dreamed up in this universe, and I loved every minute of writing her. So much so that I couldn't seem to kill her...

I was sad to see her die, but she survived for six additional books than was my intention. I thought she would die when Zabasha came back to power, but instead she became a vessel for her spirit, and then survived that to live for a whole additional arc. That's how much I loved her.

I didn't even want to kill her this time, but the moment her arm burnt to a crisp, I knew she would not survive. That wasn't in the outline, and I decided on it in the moment because up until then I was still trying to make her survive. Turning that screw made it impossible for her to survive, and I'm glad I did it, even though it was difficult.

And if I killed Red, I would have to kill Nimue, too. I'm not sure how I feel about Nimue's death. She was a constant in these books, every bit as much a force for change than Rose, Red, or Chelle. However, Nimue's fate was sealed as with Red's. Red's entire arc started with her trying to kill Nimue, and while Nimue changed throughout the books, I don't think she ever repented enough to stop Red's ire.

In fact, Red did spare Nimue after the fourth book.

She gave her a chance to change, which was more than Nimue might have deserved, but the minute that Nimue betrayed the Fairy Realm, there was only one thing that would satisfy Red, and it was Nimue's death. It would have been cruel not to give Red her justice before her death.

I loved writing Nimue maybe more than any other character. She was a chaos agent and her penchant for evil meant that I could take her places I couldn't take any other character. I thought for a moment that she would be redeemed, but even the death of the King in Yellow was not enough to wash the blood from her hands from the past 11 books.

Then you have Rose and Chelle, who finally ended up together for good. They got exactly what they wanted, which was to be together, and hopefully, exactly what you wanted. I really, really want them to have a happily ever after. One of the saddest parts about writing this series is knowing that since they are both POV characters and the book happens over dozens of planets and realms, it meant I had to pull them apart over and over again. I just want these two kids to be happy, which brings me to the future.

I am currently struggling with whether this is the end of the series. I have four more books planned, but without Red or Nimue, have I lost too big a part of the books to keep going? Besides, right now Rose and Chelle are happy, and I think maybe that is a good place to end it. I think I've satisfied everything I ever intended to do with these books.

Still, though, I bought four more covers, and have books 13-16 laid out in basic detail. When I plotted this book out, I thought this would be the end. I can't say for sure whether it will be. You will know more than me since by the time this book releases I'll have either written book 13 or moved on to something else.

I think the final arc I had planned would be really cool, but I am not sure I am ready to send Rose and Chelle into the chipper again. I often feel that way after finishing an arc though. I've lived with this one for the past eight months, and I'm excited to take a little break from it and let them live in peace and see where the muse takes me.

If I do write a fourth arc, it will be a doozy. So far, we've destroyed the Dream Realm, the Underworld, the Fairy Realm, and the Celestial Realm. Next time, we will destroy the whole universe, unless our heroines can stop it.

I hope you enjoyed this arc, and it satisfied you. I loved writing it, and I love these characters, so much so that I don't know if I want to do them the type of harm planned for them in the next arc, if there is one. Right now, there are five POV characters still alive right now in the Obsidian Spindle Saga; Rose, Chelle, Gwen, Lucy, and Queen Aine. We haven't seen a POV chapter from Gwen and Lucy for four books, and we haven't checked in with Queen Aine for eight, so it is kind of exciting to think about getting into their heads again.

I guess time will tell. Until then, happy reading.

You have finished reading The Obsidian Spindle Saga. Are you ready to dive into another portal fantasy series? Then here is a preview of Change, the first book in The Godsverse Chronicles.

CHANGE PREVIEW

Book 0 of The Godsverse Chronicles
By:
Russell Nohelty

Edited by:
Leah Lederman

Proofread by:
Katrina Roets & Toni Cox

Cover by:
Psycat Covers

Planet chart and timeline design by:
Andrea Rosales

CHAPTER ONE

I hated it when Ollie called me because it always meant a big job that took me away from home for long stretches. She was a good client, but she was all business and refused to take no for an answer.

"You don't have to go, Sadie," my girlfriend said, turning over in bed to rest her arm on my stomach. "It's the middle of the night."

The thing I hated most about Ollie calling me was that she paid too well for me to say no. "This is the last time, Leigh. I promise."

"That's what you said last time."

I slid out of bed and pulled on a pair of ripped jeans. They were tight, but the advantage of being a changeling was that you were never constrained by something as trivial as gaining or losing weight. A ripple went through my stomach, and my flabby belly cinched in on itself like I was pulled into a corset, and the extra inch it gave allowed me to button my pants.

"How much do you figure you actually weigh?" Leigh asked. "I mean, if your powers were taken away tomorrow, would you balloon up to 300 pounds, 500, or more?"

I thought for a moment as I grabbed a Led Zeppelin t-shirt I got at a concert a few years ago. I cut off the sleeves, and the holes had grown over time. Now, they drooped down to the middle of my stomach.

"Last time I looked, I was like 270 or something like that." I tapped on my stomach. "But it's all muscle, baby."

Leigh rolled her eyes. "I would kill for your power."

I leaped onto the bed and kissed her. "Please, like you don't get the benefit. I didn't see you complaining when you were being screwed by Bo Derek last week or Grace Kelly the week before that. Meanwhile, I have to make do with little old you forever."

Her eyes went wide, and she pushed me off her playfully. "And you can barely handle that."

"Ouch." I pushed myself up to stand and grabbed my heart. "That hurts, truly."

She grabbed a pillow and flung it out. "Get out of here so I can go back to sleep."

"Love you!" I shouted as I turned to the door.

"Love you too, jerk. Don't die!"

I walked into the kitchen and grabbed a box of cereal. It took a lot of calories to keep up my body, which meant shotgunning bowls of sugary cereal and fattening fast food. Even after downing two bowls of Cocoa Krispies, I would need to stop off at In-N-Out Burger for a Double-Double and a shake. Otherwise, I would quite literally fall into a pile of goo when I tried to transform.

I took the elevator down to the garage and hopped into the '74 Mustang I bought before I met Leigh. She thought it was gaudy and showy, but those were also the qualities she liked most about me, that I had a flair for the dramatic.

I looked at myself in the rearview mirror. The skin around my eyes began to sag, and I used my power to suck the bags tight to my skin again. My appearance changed every day and for every client, but I always kept it the same around Leigh, unless she asked me to change, of course. When I met her, I was a brown-haired woman with green eyes and freckles, so that's what I returned to most of the time even when I wasn't around her...unless I was on a job. That green-eyed girl was the best part of myself, and on a job, I was the worst part. I couldn't do any of the things Ollie asked of me if I looked like the woman Leigh loved.

I closed my eyes and took a breath. When I opened them again, my skin had darkened, as had my hair. My eyes were now brown and had none of the luster I kept special for Leigh. Now I was completely plain in about every way. I would blend into every crowd, an average Jane in a city filled with women determined to stand out.

I grabbed two Double-Doubles with animal-style fries and ate them as I drove down the 405 to Venice. Ollie owned homes all over the city in case of emergencies, but she spent most of her time in a small Venice bungalow on the canals. She wasn't much of a bohemian, but she liked the fact that the canal cut off attacks from one side, and the attached homes on either side meant she only had to protect one side of her house.

I parked on the street and took the stairs down to the canal. I passed the boat Ollie kept in case she needed a quick escape and knocked on the sliding glass door. Ollie never took off her sunglasses, even in the dark of night. She was pretty, with a thin face and features that could have had her featured in any number of magazines if that was her thing. Of course, if it was, then I would hate her.

She wore a leather jacket and tight jeans, and she paced

from side to side as she screamed into a phone. Her house was soundproof, but I could still see her hand flinging around and the color filling her face. When she saw me, she hung up the phone and rushed to the door.

"Thank the gods you're here," she said, pulling me inside. "I need your help."

"I assumed that was why you called me in the middle of the night."

"Is it the middle of the night?" She looked at a clock on the wall. "I suppose it is, isn't it? Well, you're here, aren't you?"

"It would seem that way."

She walked to the kitchen and pulled out a small envelope stuffed with money. She handed it to me. "For your trouble and to get you started. There's more where that came from, obviously."

I fingered the cash but didn't count it fully. "How much are we talking about?"

"If you find what I'm looking for, then a hundred grand more."

I did a double-take. "Must be dangerous."

"Not only is it dangerous," Ollie said, "it's impossible. I've called a dozen of my best people, and none of them can find what I'm looking for, which is why I called you."

"And what do I get if I can't find what you're looking for?" I said.

"Half. Win, lose, or draw."

"You must be desperate." I waited for her face to betray her bargaining position, but it never came. "I'll do it, but I want one hundred thousand either way and five hundred if I find what you're looking for."

She laughed. "You must be kidding. That's bloody extortion."

I shrugged. "If you have some other way, I can leave."

Ollie growled. "Fine, if you can put it in my hand, I'll give you five hundred, but you better deliver it on a bed of goddamn diamonds."

"I can't promise that. Besides, diamonds are gauche." A smile cracked across my face. "So, what am I looking for?"

She reached down onto the messy coffee table and pulled out a picture. "It's a knife, a dagger really. I have a client that's been tracking it for a long time but lost the scent a couple of weeks ago. He's paying me a lot of money to find it for him, but he needs it this week, or the deal is off, which doesn't give us a lot of time."

The dagger was made of black metal like I never saw before and curled into a jagged, sinewy S down to the hilt. A ruby rested at the top of the handle that looked like an eye staring out at me. I had never been creeped out by an inanimate object until that moment.

"Which is why you called on me, the best."

"And the only shapeshifter I've ever met."

It was impossible to know how many changelings existed in the world since they blended into the background so easily, but I only met a dozen or so who admitted their powers to me. There could have been millions for all I knew, but our powers were highly coveted. Many people believed they could drink our blood and steal our powers, and even though that was stupid, so was magic. I honestly didn't know if it was true or not. I never tested it.

"I'll do this job for you." I looked up at her. "But after this, I want out, Ollie. It's too much for—"

She held up her hand. "No, it's okay. I get it. I've thought about retiring enough times to get it. Just be quick about it."

"Do you have any leads?" I asked.

She pulled out a manila folder. "That's everything I know about the demon who stole it from my client. He was last seen in Brussels. I'll open a portal for you, but after that, you're on your own unless you get really stuck."

"Just like every other mission." I nodded. "I'll see you soon."

"You better." She pulled a wand from her leather jacket. "Porth i saesneg brwsel."

A light shot from the edge of her wand, and she cut open a hole in reality at the center of her living room. On the other side of it, I saw the bright light of day in a small Belgian alley.

"And Sadie," Ollie said as she stared at me from the other side of the portal, "if you want half a million dollars, don't expect me to recoup your expenses."

I stepped through the portal. "Just like every other mission."

CHAPTER TWO

Demons were notoriously hard to corner alone, as they were both incredibly strong and infinitely cagey. The most powerful demons in Hell stayed that way through conniving, back-stabbing, and deception. Those that made it up to Earth succeeded in the same way, except that they preyed on humans instead of others of their kind.

Ja'rel'vre went by Jared on the surface, and a selection of weaker demons and other monsters from Hell guarded his compound. On Earth, they masked themselves through a series of charmed objects and spells that allowed them to blend into humanity, but there was always a hint of sulfur in the air when they were around.

Usually, I would follow Jared around for a month, learning their habits before I pounced, but Ollie gave me an impossible deadline. Every minute counted, so I had to take some shortcuts that would normally be too risky for me. I liked to work in the background, only slipping in and out of a situation when I could go undetected. That was impossible in this case, but half a million dollars was enough to retire comfortably, and so risks I would normally steer away from were completely in play as long as it saved me time.

Still, unless I had a death wish, I couldn't simply waltz into Jared's compound and attack them head-on. Luckily, his dossier told me he ate out every night at a little French bistro a few miles from his house. That was as good a place to ambush him as any. I waited for his limo to leave the gated drive that guarded his mansion and sped ahead to make sure I was there when Jared entered the restaurant.

When I arrived at Chez Antonius, I saw a pretty, young waitress with a spiteful face smoking a cigarette out behind a dumpster next to the restaurant. Her eyes were light brown and with thick bangs. Half her hair was pink, and the other half blue. She stood out from everything around her and was easily the most beautiful girl I ever saw, outside of my Leigh.

I spent a little time as a waitress in my youth, and while I hated the job, the wait staff was a perfect way to infiltrate a secret meeting, so it paid to keep my skills sharp.

"Excuse me," I said in perfect French. Learning languages had been a hobby of mine for years, and I mastered three dozen languages and was proficient in twenty more.

"What do you want?" the waitress growled at me. Her name tag said Claudette.

"I have a proposition for you if you'll hear it."

She took a drag of her cigarette. "I am not interested in sex with you."

"It's not a sex thing."

"Then I still want to be alone."

I pulled a wad of cash out of my pocket. It paid to keep a few thousand dollars handy in local currency. "Are you sure?"

Belgian waitresses made good money, but a hundred thousand Belgian Francs was more than even they made in a night. "You have my attention."

I waved the wad of cash. "I will give you all this money if you leave now, and don't come back for an hour."

Her eyes narrowed at me. "So you want me to get fired, then?"

"Not quite, just disappear into the ether. In an hour, you can come back, and it will be like this never happened, I promise."

She scoffed. "Matteau is a dick. He'll chew me out if I leave for ten minutes. It's nearly the dinner rush."

"Maybe." I shrugged as I eyed the limo pulling up and a short, fat man in a three-piece suit waddled into the restaurant, flanked by two gorgeous women on each arm. "But is a hundred thousand francs enough to put up with him chewing you out?"

Her eyes rolled up in her head as she thought about it. "No, but two hundred thousand would."

That was almost four thousand dollars, more than she probably made in two months. I smiled as I dipped into the reserves in my pocket. "Consider it done. Give me that cigarette and your apron."

She shrugged and did as she was told. "Whatever."

"Oh, and tell me about the fat man that just walked inside."

"He's annoying, and he's in love with me. Sometimes I let him feel me up when I need some money."

That was good. I could use that. "Thank you."

"Are you going to kill him?" My eyes went wide as she smirked. "I don't care. I just want to know what is worth two hundred thousand francs for an hour of my time."

"Just don't come back for an hour."

I handed her the wad of cash, and she walked off into the night. I used the cigarette to get the DNA I needed to transform into a perfect replica of the waitress. When I had the apron over my neck, I slid inside the back door. The kitchen was in chaos as cooks moved back and forth between the stoves and the pans, swirling sauces and braising beef. The smell of it made me salivate, but there would be time for that later.

"Where were you?" a tall, grizzled man with a bushy mustache growled as I walked inside. "I said a cigarette break, not an afternoon nap."

"I'm sorry," I replied, moving faster. "It wasn't very busy. I thought I could have five minutes to myself. How silly of me."

I made the assumption that Claudette would not take any guff from her boss, and from the small smile on his face, I figured I was right. "Jared is back, and you know he only likes you to wait on him."

I growled, "I will take care of it."

"Don't take him to the bathroom like last time, or I'll have to fire you."

"Please," I replied. "You love me too much to fire me."

"That is where you are very wrong." He pointed to a tray of hors d'oeuvres, and I picked it up before sliding out of the kitchen and into the front of the house. The tables were dimly lit, and there were very few guests inside, but the ruckus from Jared's table filled every corner, drowning out the silence. Demons were loud and disgusting.

"Good evening," I said as I placed down the tray.

Jared slapped my ass, and I just about cut his throat, but I kept my composure and turned to him. "What did I tell you about that?"

Jared smiled. "Only in private?"

My eyes narrowed before I remembered what Claudette had told me. "Are you prepared to put your money where my mouth is?"

A capricious grin rose on his face. "I have plenty of money, if you will let me use it to find your mouth, I would reward you handsomely."

I finished putting the last of the appetizers down on the table. "Let me get us a drink, and then I will meet you in the bathroom."

I brought the tray to the bar and slid it to a young man who looked at me with disgust. "Two limoncellos."

He turned and grabbed a bright yellow bottle. "You can't mean to let him—not again. Not after what Matteau said last time."

I shot a look at him to shut up. "Why do you think he keeps coming here? For the overpriced food or your charming company? No, he comes because I make him come. Don't forget it." He handed the drinks to me. "Judge me silently from now on."

I took the drinks and pulled a small vial out of my pocket. I kept holy water on hand in case I came into contact with any demons. Spraying it into their faces would give you a chance to escape but pouring it down their throat was a quick way to send them into an early grave, and they wouldn't rematerialize in Hell, either.

I dripped a couple of drops into each drink and watched Jared disappear into the bathroom. I waited a second before joining him. He pulled me close before the door even swung shut, and I swallowed the urge to vomit as the sulfur hit my nostrils. Demons weren't always disgusting to look at, but Jared was little more than a mass of fat made human, and when he grabbed me, his body undulated like a bowl of Jell-O.

"Come here, my Belgian flower."

I held my hands into the air. "Ah ah. First, we drink."

He growled at me, his hot, disgusting breath hitting my face and sending a shiver down my back. "Don't keep me waiting, ma chérie."

"Not waiting, just anticipating." I opened my mouth and downed the drink before holding the other one over his mouth. He smirked devilishly before opening his gullet and letting me pour a drink down his throat. "There we go."

I slipped out of his grasp and placed the drinks on the counter. By the time I turned back, the tincture had taken effect, and he was on his knees, wheezing. "What—what have you done—"

I turned back into my previous form and smiled at him. "I have a question for you, and if you answer, then I'll give you the antidote."

"I'll kill you!" he screamed.

"You might, and you might succeed, but without the antidote, you won't even die. You'll simply cease to be."

He fell to the ground. "What—what do you want to know? Hurry—hurry!"

"Where is the dagger you stole? The sinewy one made of black metal. And don't play dumb with me. I know you have it."

He choked out every word. "Haaad—Had it—I don't—I don't have it anymore—"

I snarled at him. "I'm not stupid, demon. I know you don't have it. I want to know where it went."

He shook his head fiercely. "I don't—"

I held up my hand. "You don't have time to lie. So, tell me the truth, right now. You're running out of time."

He coughed, trying to regain his breath. "Kirkorov. The KGB spook. He took it from me. Then disappeared behind the Iron Curtain. I can't—I haven't been—" He coughed. "Please, give me the antidote! Please. That is the truth."

"I believe you." I stood up and chuckled. "The thing is, I don't have it."

I stepped over him as he flailed on the ground, writhing against his imminent death. I smiled as I passed the bartender, who heard the screams and didn't know what to do.

"Call an ambulance, I think," I said as I slipped out the door. It was going to be tough for Claudette, but she could dry her tears on all the money I gave her.

A scream cut through the air as the bartender's face dropped. "Did you really—"

But by the time he turned around to look at me, I was gone into the ether. It was about to get messy, and I needed to get gone before all of Brussels was on my tail.

CHAPTER THREE

"You do realize, even for me, getting into the Soviet Union isn't cake, right?" Ollie told me when I called her with the information I got from Jared. "Also, I thought I told you not to call collect anymore."

"Oh, I'm sorry. Did you not want to get updated about this dagger you are up my butt about finding?"

"No, I do. I just want you to foot the bill."

"While you're complaining, you're wasting precious time, and time is money. Are you going to help me or not?"

She grumbled something to herself, which I could only assume wasn't polite since I couldn't hear it. "Take the next flight to West Berlin. I'll have my friend Dimitri meet you at the airport. He'll get you the papers you need to cross the border at Checkpoint Charlie."

"That's what I wanted to hear. Thanks."

"Don't thank me, just find that dagger," she said and hung up.

Belgium and Germany shared a border, so it was relatively easy to catch a cheap flight from Brussels to Berlin. Reagan worked hard to cool the tensions between the USSR and the west, and we all had a lot of hope that Gorbachev would be easier to work with than Chernenko, but the Berlin Wall still stood as a huge indicator that the Soviet Union was not interested in playing nice with the west. Getting through the Iron Curtain wasn't easy, even for somebody who knew Russian and could shapeshift into any form they wanted. However, the one thing working in my favor was that few people wanted to break into the Soviet Bloc. Most people were trying to break out. Of course, that was because it was a nightmarish hellscape…and I was walking right into the belly of the beast.

When I landed in West Berlin, I found a tall, svelte man in a long coat and a thick beard who held up a sign reading "PITA" for "pain in the ass," which was the sort of joke Ollie would make for me.

"Are you Dimitri?" I asked, walking up to him.

"Da," he replied. "You must be the pita."

I chuckled. "Most people call me Sadie."

"Ah," he said. "This is some sort of joke, then?"

I nodded. "Something like that."

I didn't pack more than a backpack, so we made our way out of the airport without stopping off at baggage claim and into a small, black car. I was lucky I packed light because little more than my backpack would have fit into the boot of the car.

"You have not been to Moscow before, da?" Dimitri asked with stern words.

"No, I haven't," I replied. "Is it nice?"

"Absolutely not," Dimitri said harshly. "Nothing about the Soviets is nice. You must be mad to want to go there."

"It's part of a job. I couldn't say no if I tried."

"Your job is very bad, then." He sighed. "Though, what would I expect from somebody who knows Ollie?"

When we could see the Berlin Wall in the distance, he pulled to a stop. Dimitri reached over me and pulled a bunch of papers out of the glove compartment. "I don't have more than a passport, but Ollie says you are a master of disguise, so it shouldn't be a problem for you."

I looked down at the passport, focusing on the picture of the husky woman staring back at me who I needed to impersonate. She had a hard face with thick jowls. Her face was expressionless, which helped my ability to turn into her.

"You don't have a piece of her hair, do you? Or a flake of skin?"

He shook his head. "Are you crazy? Why would I collect such things?"

"No reason." I would have liked a piece of hair to make the disguise more believable, but I would have to make my best guesses and hope it was good enough.

"Did you find Kirkorov?"

He nodded. "He lives in Moscow. He heads a program to acquire magical weapons that can finally win their war with the west."

"They must be desperate if they think a dagger is going to be their salvation."

He looked at me, expressionless. "Desperation is our natural state. We live with it like an old friend."

"Wow, that is bleak, even for me."

He didn't seem to acknowledge me as he continued, "I have arranged for my contact in Moscow to meet you at the Alexandr's Bar in the Mozhaysky district. There is a map I included with the rest of your things. It will show you the location. She will meet you in three days' time." He pulled a wad of cash from the inside of his coat. "Ollie says you are good for this much, but you might need more."

I grabbed several thousand dollars out of my pocket and handed him enough to exchange with him. "Thanks."

"This will get you to Moscow. Just follow the route through Poland and Belarus. All roads lead to Moscow from here." He got out of the car, and I did the same. He extended his hand. "Good luck. Do not get caught. The Soviets are not kind to spies."

"I will take that under advisement."

"See that you do." He patted the car. "This is a good car. It will get you to Moscow, even through the cold, oppressive winter."

I exchanged places with him and drove forward toward the checkpoint. Dimitri did not wait to see me go. He turned on his heels and disappeared from sight seconds after I pulled forward.

The Berlin Wall, at least from the West, was covered in graffiti and trash. It looked like it could be blown over by a stiff wind, and yet the guard towers on the far side spoke loudly that it was not to be trifled with, at least on the Soviet side.

Dimitri sent me through the most famous of the checkpoints into the Soviet Union, Checkpoint Charlie. It was generally used by Allied troops and foreigners, so I hoped they would be less strict than others, which were just for nationals. Before I reached the gate, I took a long moment to look at the passport of the woman I was impersonating. Her name was Galina Petrov, and she was 57 years old.

It was always more painful to maneuver my body into a new form without a strand of DNA to use, and the wider the person, the more I had to stretch my body to accommodate their figure. Luckily, I had eaten a meaty lunch to aid with the process. I stretched myself horizontally quite a bit to impersonate Galina, and by the time I was done, I looked at myself through gritted teeth. I held the passport next to my face and thought it was close enough to match the blurry black and white picture.

I took my car through to the gate, where a stern-looking soldier with a tall wool hat stared at me. "Papers," he said once in English, then in German, then in Russian. I understood all three, but I was only proficient in Russian, not fluent in it.

I handed the soldier the papers and nodded at him. "Here you go."

He looked over the papers for a long moment. "You are supposed to enter through Checkpoint Alpha."

"I know," I said, trying my best to hide my stilted Russian. "I have very little petrol, and I hoped to make it home before getting more."

The soldier growled at me. In the old days, in the years right after the war when the wall was erected, my insolence never would have stood, but these days nobody had the heart to keep the fight going anymore on either side of the divide, so the soldier simply rolled his eyes. "Don't let it happen again."

The gate rose, and I continued. "Thank you."

I put the car in gear and continued across the demilitarized zone into the Soviet Union. The sign at the exit to the checkpoint told me it was exactly 1,793 Kilometers to Moscow. It was the only city on the sign, despite there being hundreds between there and Berlin. Dimitri was right. All roads led to Moscow.

Did you like that preview, then get it for free today.

ABOUT THE AUTHOR

Russell Nohelty is a USA Today bestselling author, publisher, and speaker. He is the author of dozens of novels and graphic novels including The Godsverse Chronicles, The Obsidian Spindle Saga, and Ichabad Jones: Monster Hunter. He has a very entertaining newsletter, which you can join at www.russellnohelty.com. He lives in Los Angeles with his wife and dogs.

Get one of my favorite books for free at:
www.russellnohelty.com/mail
Substack:
https://authorstack.substack.com
Bookbub:
https://www.bookbub.com/profile/russell-nohelty

www.ingramcontent.com/pod-product-compliance
Lightning Source LLC
Chambersburg PA
CBHW040222170726

48295CB00014B/771